POLAND FREEZE FRAMES

POLAND FREEZE FRAMES

JANUSZ ANDERMAN
Translated by Nina Taylor

readers international

CONTENTS

Freeze Frame One

The country is fading on the maps, bit by bit withering away; the outlines of the borders blur, soften, spread out in all three directions of the world, so it becomes impossible for sensitive fingertips to feel them any more; his town disintegrated and can be found only in the dull scraps of his memory.

The streets end unexpectedly in army barricades; the tree, despite the proclamation of spring, is dry, leafless, the house on Przechodnia Street is deserted.

The addresses in the notebook go blank or crumple away; life according to the rules remains; behind the high prison walls — only there does hope survive.

Barbed air wounds the lungs, people forget the future, their world has the short life of film clips, notes lost on scattered cards.

The town is gasping for breath, and a woman in a washed-out smock getting out of the official black Volga on the main road looks desperately around, unable to remember where she was supposed to deliver the bowl of soup she carries on a plastic tray...

— Sipping tea is one thing, but this is something else — the soldier growls, emphatically adjusting his machine gun...

Sinking Wells

I stood by the pump. Dug in firmly with my feet. My left leg thrust back, rooted in a clump of dried grass. The right one flexed at the knee, freer, so that it did not have to bear my weight. The left leg did that job without so much as a tremor.

I looked ahead; there were braided knots of veins bulging on the backs of my hands. Branching off in every direction, they wrapped the entire hand in a loving gesture and disappeared only at the fingers, where they ran more deeply. They proved the importance of hands, they were their own confirmation. There was an uneasy stir and pulsing beneath the skin and the strain caused bright spots to appear at the wrists. Fingers, wrists, shoulders, the hands were tired. They felt today's work and that of previous days. They felt every minute.

The meadow was still ablaze in the heat; without a breath of wind the dry grass moved like green tongues of fire.

…well, so they covered my face with a mask, I couldn't speak, 'cos I mean I had my face covered, I just motioned with my head to show I was suffocating, when they told me to take a deep breath I felt I was suffocating, I motioned with my head and it all went blank; suddenly they woke me up and then I was surprised I couldn't fall asleep, tell me, and the operation was over; I didn't even know when I'd dropped off, 'cos when they put that mask over my face I couldn't utter a word, you see I had my face covered, only I motioned with my head to show I was suffocating, when they told me to breathe deep I felt I was suffocating, I motioned with my head and it all went blank; so when I woke up...

— P-pull, cuntie — the voice seemed to come from under the earth. My fingers tightened their grip on the warm iron of the winch.

— It's running, cuntie — I turned more slowly, more rhythmically. The tin bucket loaded with sand sailed out above the last ring. Holding the winch in my right hand, I leaned over to the left and pulled the bucket away in the direction of the mound of earth. There I tipped out the load; the sand was moist, and a pool of muddy water had gathered at the bottom of the bucket.

— It's running onto me, cuntie. We'll have to use the hood — came a shuffling and scraping out of the dark. Then he appeared. He supported his shoulders and legs against the rings and, twisting about like a worm, worked his way up through the well-shaft towards the torrid daylight.

— One day you'll have a fall, Mr. Oblegorek — I said.

— If I'd wanted to fall I'd have killed myself a hundred times already. Think I'm fool enough for that? We'll have to use the hood, seeing as you're pouring mud over me head.

— Sorry.

— Sorry, sorry. When we was building a road once with me brother-in-law Wysocki it was sorry sir sorry sir all the time. There was five of us lads and so — please sir. thank you, sir, and whenever one pulled out a pack of Sport fags Do have one of mine, oh no really do try one of mine. Well so we was breaking up stone and one of 'em hammered me brother-in-law Wysocki's finger instead, and he said look where you're 'itting, you son-of-a-bitch, and that was the end of the please sirs. So just you stop apologizing, we'll use the hood.

He sat down on a small mound of moist sand that had been freshly excavated from inside the hot earth, pulled off his boots and squeezed out his foot-cloths. He set his short-helved shovel aside on the grass for it to dry out.

— Never leave the shovel at the bottom. See what I mean, the rust gets it. But a boot's a boot. You're safe in your boots. Now bare hands is different. I was cutting chaff once and stuck me finger in. One blow and it was a gonner. I yelled for the old woman whose chaff I was cutting; I says, see if there ain't a finger in that chaff. Well and so there is, she says. I pressed it on, and tied it up in a rag and thinks, if it works it works, if it don't it don't. Agony I might say. In the morning I went to the lady doc, she undid the bandage and examined it, all right then, if it heals it heals, if it don't it don't. Then she smeared it with some yellow muck. And I've still got it. That finger there. It's not much good at bending, but it can still lift a table. Just the thing for well-sinking. Anyway I was a born well-sinker, cuntie. Didn't grow on purpose, see.

... the red vocalist sings a Parisian tango, the crowd moves in rhythm, ominously; a woman in a white cap and pompom; sweat streams down her, her buttocks wrapped in elastic trousers; a little man in a red lace shirt nestles his face between the woman's breasts and shuffles at her side, and she holds on to his sideburns...

I propped myself against the well-casing, as it gave off some coolness and shade for my shoulders. But not much, and it no longer nursed my legs. We hadn't been sitting for long, and the shadow still hadn't budged.

— Mister Oblegorek, that well could be a sundial.

— What you mean?

— Only you'd have to sink the rings aslant. At an angle.

— A slanting well? Must be the heat today that makes you talk such rubbish. Let's get on. It's a decent enough job, only the day's too long.

— The day's not that bad. It's bearable.

...when we took the old fruit we all stood round her, she was on the trolley on the way to the operating theatre and basically she was gone, she just held out a hand and mumbled; I'd like to go on a train journey, a long long way just for fun, I'd like to take a train; we were all waiting and thinking she was dead or whatever, when they brought her up at last, eyes shut, so we all touched her, still warm, therefore alive, and so on right through the night; the operation, when they put that mask on my face I felt I was suffocating and I motioned with my head because my face was covered...

— It's the night that's too long, Mister Oblegorek.

— In the night you sleep with a woman. Or you run round begging with your prick. Let's get on. When a bloke earns a bit of money it does something for his spirits. And the bitch wouldn't give a hundred-zloty note for a good building job. She said no, she'd have none of it. I wanted to take her twenty years back, but she wouldn't look at me. I hadn't a bean. See, and now she's buried her old man, and I'll not be having her now. But in those days I was running after her like a mad dog. She was, you might say, badly dispositioned towards my person. Now I'm the artful one these days. If I wasn't, I wouldn't be sporting a nylon raincoat. But in those days I was like a mad dog. Like I always had her before my eyes. A strapping woman she was. Today she's just a runt. And she wouldn't give a hundred-zloty note for a good job. Once me brother-in-law Wysocki and me was building a barn. We had a carpenter with us, and me brother-in-law's a decent fellow 'cos he knows how to drink. Cuntie, we went and asked the farm-lady for a hundred-zloty note to brick up in a corner for good luck and what have you. Cuntie, she didn't want to at first, but she did in the end. We stuck that hundred-note in the foundation, gave it a splash of cement, and when the woman went off, cuntie, we whipped the bank note out again and sent the lad for some wine. He brought five bottles and there was enough change for sixty cigs — just fifty groszy short. Then the carpenter paid for another round, we knocked it all back. And it went on like that for six days. The carpenter took an advance of a thousand zlotys and we carried on drinking, then he packed up and went, because Sunday came, and so we never saw him again.

I stood by the pump. Dug in firmly with my feet. My left leg thrust back, rooted in a clump of dried grass. The right one flexed at the knee, freer, so that it did not have to bear my weight. The left leg did that job without so much as a tremor.

I was watching the winch. Not the vast small world behind my back. An ugly world where Sunday is like a stain of mildew... what's to drink; why tell you, you always order the same, there's beer; someone says, what a thought, one could say that those trees die standing; I don't want to be a snob by which I mean to follow public opinion, but there are two camps, one against, and that is contra, the other for, and that means for; please sir, a beer, I'm feeling low, if you've finished your food kindly vacate your place; people distort and exaggerate; I run a sulfur mag and when I want to go somewhere I just say that I'm going and I go, I write about foremen and the like, just for reading the papers I've got more cash in hand than you; please sir, but do tell me, are you a prince or aren't you, only please tell me, my dear; I'm from pretty good stock; but are you a prince, mate, or aren't you...

The landscape passes by along the train. The day breaks out, then subsides and holds steady. Oblegorek introduces me with a shout:

— Grandpa, I've found a helper. He thumbed a ride out here.

— So put it under the pear tree then — he replies. And the next day I was sitting in the pine trees against the sun and I could see Oblegorek's shadow. He walked round the meadow on his wide-apart legs, and stretched his hands out before him like a blind man. He was holding a forked birch branch carved of that gentlest of trees and slowly he stumped forward. His white brimmed well-sinker's hat was tilted back on his head. He was absorbed and tense, and the veins sprouted out on his temples like little brooks from under the brim.

— Jesus, Jesus — groaned the farm woman crouching behind me as, hard-handed, she blessed the hot air in four parts.

The heat was slumbering. The dried grass did not bind the earth together, and it now rose in clouds of dust from under the impatient stamping boots.

— May the Lord God cripple that motherfucker. May He strike him, the monster — growled the widow, tearing pieces of living flesh from the body of her neighbour who had barred the way to his well, that she now had to pay these thousands.

— May the plague take him, amen.

The birch withe twitched in Oblegorek's hands.

Finally it curved down towards the parched earth, and he drew violently to a halt.

— I feel water here, this is where we'll bore.

— Jesus — groaned the widow.

— I feel water — he repeated and sat down on the edge of a hillock. He pulled out cigarettes, and the widow kept shaking her head wrapped in thoughts as heavy as the heat.

And then the first ring was lowered into the friable soil, and I had nothing to do. Oblegorek was fixing it, excavating as he went.

— Then you see me brother-in-law Wysocki, cuntie, was sinking a well. I only came to do the explosives, 'cos his son worked in the stone-pit and took as much dyno as he fancied. We dug out thirty metres in the rock, there was no water, but I thought, cuntie, hope no one falls in 'cos brother-in-law stinted on the timbering. Well, and it was brother-in-law Wysocki who fell in. I come running along, cuntie, and asks how he fell. On his head they said. So I says to me brother-in-law's son, better earth it over, you'll save on the funeral, besides it'ud be a sin to drink from the well now. No question of that he says, not at all, cuntie, must bring him up. We sent one man down, because me brother-in-law's son didn't want to go down there himself, no way. But how to fish him out? They tie him under the armpits, then up shoot the arms, cuntie, and out he slips. Well then, I suggest tying him by the head, but then I thinks when the persecutor comes along he'll say we hung him. So we roped up his leg, I pulled, but the blood gushed out of him again, and the fellow at the bottom shouted that he's swamped in blood. And brother-in-law Wysocki's a decent bloke, 'cos he's a good drunk. He knew how to get drunk alright. And so thirty metres was wasted.

Oblegorek was standing in the first ring. It was not deep, so his head in the well-sinker's hat stuck out over the edge. And then it began to recede into the cavity, vanished altogether, and I stood with my left leg supporting and turned the warm metal of the winch. I looked in front of me. At the blazing meadow and above it.

Oblegorek is drilling in the soil; he digs stubbornly, and when I lean over the ring of darkness I cannot even see him. I only hear his voice, which seems to come from under the earth.

— She didn't want me, cuntie, so now she's buried her old man. And I was after her like a dog after a bitch, with my prick a-begging.

He drilled and penetrated deep, and up above I took the load, a bucketful of moist shavings. When the ring drew level with the surface, Oblegorek emerged from the darkness; he unhitched the bucket, placed one leg in the cable-loop, leaned the other leg and then his shoulder against the wall. I gave one turn of the winch, he sought support higher up, then the next turn and the next support, until he appeared in the sun. We fixed the next ring. Oblegorek did not stop to rest. He did not even sit with a fag and smoke it out with his usual sense of purpose. He did not squeeze the water out of his foot-cloths, only went back into the darkness and drilled. In a passion for this living soil.

— And I was after her like a cur after a bitch. With my prick a-begging.

I looked in front of me. At the blazing meadow and above it. Towards the blue strip of pines and on the left towards a stand of young birches, the loveliest of trees, covered in bark warm as the skin on animal bellies. We looked for water, drilling to the source. My gaze did not reach beyond the blue strip of pines. They were the horizon. And those gentle birches.

No words could attack here. I was shielded by the calm of the meadow. Couldn't hear the barman standing with the shocked face, his torso cut in two by the metal tabletop.

…Jeez,…Jeez, it's you, but I had a scare, they said you'd been killed in a crash, the car a write-off, but maybe they weren't talking about you, I can't remember now, jeez… I thought to myself, such a highbrow type, I thought to myself at once, as soon as I ever saw you here, it was a load of codswallop; do you know Lieutenant Smyk, wha', I'm buying a whole bottle, wha', I was doing the boilers for a certain professor and he tells me to do one and I did, do you know Lieutenant Smyk? I'll take a whole bottle; he stumbles over and like Christ falls spread-eagled on the wet tiles of the bog; the waitress swipes the client across his face, you've been asleep long enough, you know me madam from an honest day's work, and I know you from a dishonest one; what's that, the restaurant's about to close, the whores 'll be round; I can tell you everything about yourself, mister, I'm a fortune-teller, a sort of clairvoyant, by the by, throw us some coppers for a beer...

Pray that they never drag me stoned from a taxi. That I never hold a nosegay in my hands and stammer, long live, long live. That a frightened taxi driver never mutters who's going to pay for the puke, who's going to pay for cleaning up the puke...

The maidenly skin of the gentle birches on the horizon. And the dark blue splash of pines.

— Found it. There's a source, cuntie... — cried Oblegorek twisting his way from one ring to the next towards the light. His trousers were wet above his boots. — Found it. When you look at the sky from below you can see stars in broad daylight. I'm stunned, cuntie. Last time I saw stars from a well.

We extracted the first bucket. The water was yellow and muddy. Opaque.

— We'll have to pull lots of muck out before it's clear — Oblegorek said reflectively as we sat by the scrubbed table of white planks.

— I'm so glad you've come, I was beginning to think you'd got lost — Grandpa fretted about the parlour, spreading his arms like a grey moth knocking against the walls. — *The Courier*, do you think it's a good paper?

There was a bottle on the table.

— It doesn't stink of rotgut. Grandpa distilled it three times.

— Have some cold meat — he pushed the black pudding, looking like caviar, in my direction. There was bread, mustard, tea. Everything was there. The white planks of the freshly scrubbed table.

— It popped out small and hairy, half-pig, half-goat, half-man — Grandpa mumbled. — That's the child she produced. It was in *The Courier*. Is the lemon good?

— And how... — Oblegorek was opening a second bottle and was hunched over the table.

— Now that's what I'd — he moved up closer. He jerked his head back, then splashed the rest onto the floor and put the glass aside. — The widow lives near here. We could travel a long way to sink another well, but we don't have to. Know what we'll do? We'll chuck a dead cat down her well. Then it'll have to be earthed over for fear of the plague. I've got just the carcass. And we'll drill another well for her nearby. I've got just the carcass. We'll throw it down her well. Only first, we've got to choose a muddy one and only when it comes up clear...

I filled my glass, knocked it back and threw the rest onto the floor. I pushed my glass aside and lit a cigarette.

— And we'll sink another well. Why travel far when there's work at hand. I've got just the carcass and we'll dig...

— I shan't be able to sink any more wells — I said with a laugh. — Must be going.

— What? Didn't I pay you enough? I thought we'd hit it off...

— It's not that. You pay good money.

— Then what's the bother?

— No bother. I hadn't told you but I must be off. You'll have to look for water with someone else. That's life.

— What? Did you hear, Grandpa? Leaving us, he is.

— So put it under the pear tree then — he replied.

1973

Freeze Frame Two

That December day they wanted to put flowers by the ship-yard gate, in memory of their dead of eleven years ago, but armoured cordons stopped them, and they could see the approaching buses only from a distance above the domes of helmets; they saw people getting off and bustling camera-men; they observed those people laying elaborate wreaths of artificial flowers for their own victims.

That first day, the television newscasters could be differentiated from the audience by their tight-fitting uniforms; the notes they held low in their fingers and glanced at made them talk mechanically; the words rolled in the white glow of the spotlights, long wrinkles on their foreheads; there were people among us who consciously sought to cause unrest, so that Polish blood would be spilled. One day history will sentence them harshly and severely for sowing discord, obstinacy, irresponsibility, lack of imagination. Their consciences will be stained by Polish blood. They should be made to face the mothers of the killed Wujek miners,* in the name of what cause did they push for confrontation? They ought to be made to look into the eyes of the victims' mothers.

— Let us bow our heads before these unnecessary deaths — the talking notes rattle, the heads of the newscasters lowered as if fearing a sudden blow.

In the room next to the television studio, the bookkeeper fills in the last lines of the wage-list.

That first night, the overcrowded prisons did not sleep, nor did a host of army sentinels...

Wujek Mine — where seven miners died resisting martial law in December 1981.

Night Shift in Emergency

Down the airless tunnel of the hospital corridor a trolley moved silently on rubber wheels. On it a man lay pinned down by the sinewy hands of the ward attendants, struggling to raise himself, shouting into the closed space, spare me, you butchers, bleed your guts out, have mercy!

His head, suddenly quiet, dropped back on the stained oil-cloth; he pulled it strenuously away from under the strong fingers of the women and continued his pleading in a scream that bounced off the walls of the corridor like sparks.

The doors of the elevator slammed and the voice was trapped in the shaft, its gloom dispersed by the husky laughter of the operator; with one hand he worked the lever, while the other wandered towards the ward attendant's crotch, shielded by her grey rag of a uniform.

A young doctor rushed into the ward and glanced round rapaciously as if counting his inventory; there were not many patients yet and he eyed the recumbent figures with an air of reproach, as though they had let him down. His gaze wore the conviction that one clean stroke of the scalpel can alter a man's life.

He circulated along the narrow passages between the beds, taking a close look at the patients before their long journey to the operating theatre.

With a razor in her slender fingers a nurse went up to the inert and flabby body of a man, could you please shave for the operation.

— So long as I don't nick myself — the man whispered, his forehead flecked with drops of sweat. He slowly twisted over onto his side, peeled down his pyjama bottoms and guided the blade over his belly. His skin sounded like torn parchment. Two convalescents, recovered since the last shift, were playing pontoon, while keeping a close eye on the world around them. A youngster lay on the bed next to them; there was no sign of suffering in his eyes, which were covered by spongy, loaf-like swellings.

— You, balloon-head, two more have already croaked it in that shirt of yours. It's got two seams. That means it's been split open twice on a stiff. Pontoon — he cried, after a glance at his cards.

The boy raised his head, but could not see his shirt, so he simply fingered the two seams which stretched from his neck down towards his belly.

The first patient to have been operated on during that shift was wheeled into the ward. As in some ritual, the nurses stretched the body onto the bed and meticulously covered the feet with the pillow they had removed from beneath the resting head. The bulb of the drip-feed swayed

above the bedding, filtering light over the patient's motionless hands.

— Don't sleep, don't sleep, how do you feel...

He dwelt on the question at length, how do I feel, how
do I feel.

— I'm dead.

The young doctor ushered in the next trolley in procession. Lay the old boy on this one — Hey, grandad, so we
meet again, how about chopping off the other leg?

— Give him a good look over, then get him out and onto
the operating table.

A nurse confusedly wrapped the thin body in the tentacle
wires that joined it to the electrocardiogram.

— How can I connect you when you haven't got a leg?
How can I connect you?

— But I can feel my leg. I can still feel it. My leg. He
turned his head towards the pillow of the bed next door
—What're you here for? I've been around these hospitals you
know.

His neighbour listened avidly, joy mounting in his torpid
eyes.

— Pretty sickness you've got there. I had me leg off here
not long ago. It's a decent place, real OK. I waited a whole
week for the emergency ward. Just to get back here. This
time I'm in for cancer. That's how it is. Just as I get used
to life without a leg, have a few drinks, manage not to care
any more. I've done my bit of boozing and dancing after all.
It's been twelve days now I've gone without food, so a bloke
begins to feel run down.

The young doctor chivvied the nurse, who was awkwardly plucking out the hairs on the old man's belly.

— Leave his prick, can't you? Finish prepping him and get him down to the theatre.

The convalescents tore their eyes away from their cards, while you're at it, nurse, give him something to remember in heaven. The girl's face was in flames and her fingers instinctively clutched the uniform which was half-open above her breasts.

A yellow stain the shape of Asia spread on the patient's bedcover. His hands had dropped, dragged down by the weight of the urine-bottle.

After a couple of hours the old man's bed is occupied again, and another mouth emerges from under the dressings like a flower, complaining to the radiator.

— Oh Jesus, oh jesu, ojesu, ojes, ojee.

— Sister. What's happened to the old boy. His bed's been taken.

— Wa'. Gone to another ward.

A solitary shoe, discarded memory of a leg, protrudes from under the bed.

The Gipsy dropped dead tonight, says the ward attendant, and burst out laughing.

— His missis brought 'im a chicken. Must have nicked it from some hen-coop. And he bunged it under his blanket. Ate the whole bloody thing. He pegged out on the spot. Well, I mean really. The second day after his op. Fairly stuffed himself he did.

An old man presses twenty zlotys into her hungry palm; treat yourself, go on. And could I have the bed pan, begging your pardon, Miss?

Coiled in a blue dressing-gown I stand in the corridor peering through the glazed doors at the young doctor who has just performed an operation, who now smokes a cigarette and talks to the nurse in the duty-room. He leans his palm against the wall above her head, and the girl hugs herself with her arms, emphasizing for his benefit the breasts under her overalls.

The young doctor notices me, well now then, are you going to sign the consent form?

— No. Don't you count on it.

— Now try a rational approach. Really it's only a minor operation. You'll be good as new. Decide now while I'm asking politely.

— Out of the question.

The thin scalpel reflects bright outside the window. In the street the engine of the night bus rumbles.

Two ticket collectors can be seen dragging a man out of the bus. He resists. They twist his arms and drag him under the street-lamp which struggles to emit some light.

I return to the ward and pass by the bursting drip-feeds. A student nurse puts a chair by the old man's bed.

She sits down, wraps herself in her grey cape and delicately unfolds the membrane of a newspaper.

— Nurse, do you know the joke about the guy who went to hospital with a dislocated prick? — the convalescents ask, setting their cards aside.

They gaze at her with lustful eyes. With a fixed unflinching stare they carve her up between them, each grabbing his share. Tomorrow they'll no longer stack the cards in equal parts.

The girl bows her head over the film listings. Her hair smothers her face and covers the blush in her cheeks like powder.

— And have you heard the one about the monk's hood? Like to hear it?

— Is it saucy? — she shyly ventures.

—You like them spicy. Don't kid me ... A lull descends on the ward.

— It's the two from the other ward — the attendants whisper.

Outside the window the town flickers before daybreak; the houses tremble slightly, the last women from the station close up like prayer books.

Workers crawl to their factories, whose chimneys have swallowed a mouthful of rainwater.

At dawn a pretty nurse comes running into the ward.

— Pee, pee, why haven't you peed for the samples yet? Quick now!

The young doctor ends his shift and will soon be back in his office, sifting out patients. He is out of his white uniform. Over his shoulders he wears a suede jacket, warm as a moist hand.

— Why aren't you sleeping?

— Why do you ask?

— Well, what about the operation? Just for interest's sake.

— There's not going to be any operation.

— You'll end up badly then. In a couple of days you'll be singing a different tune.

— Don't be ridiculous.

The young doctor jerks out his left leg, his palm clenches hedgehog-like into a fist which he lands in the pit of my stomach.

I bend as if bowing in thanks; my mouth fails to inhale.

The young doctor runs down the steps and out of the hospital.

Once in the street he glances back up at the window and sees me. Then he slams his car door and roars off into town.

Unbandaged for dressing, the patient's head wakes up like a hard day.

Hands flounder towards the empty strawberry jam jars. Cards with surnames written in rounded, girlish lettering are stuck on them.

Moans rise in the ward. In the changing-room the nurses pare skin-tight white overalls from their bodies, scanning one another with jealous glances.

— The one with the big tits is on duty today — says the convalescent.

— The one with 'em bursting right out of her uniform. Sister, how many have snuffed it in emergency to date?

— What? What's today? — the old man comes out of his drugged sleep. A day beggaring description begins.

1975

Freeze Frame Three

...These women who age and go grey in a few months...

These women who move skilfully through the tunnels of clothes, tins, packets and medicines which fill the glazed corridors of the monastery...

These women who perch like grey sparrows on the cartons to snatch a quick rest, who do not even think about the night.

They are making parcels for those known only by their surnames and for the orphaned families. They sit on the boxes, and the stone floor swells their voices to infinity.

— In one of the camps, the screws were beating people and ordering them to kiss their boots.

— In another, a woman has been told that her son died, but they will let her attend the funeral only if she signs the declaration of loyalty.

— A man is in hiding, so they keep coming to his mother asking where he is, and she says she has no idea, so they threaten to take her to the mortuary every Monday to look at the new bodies, just in case her son's is among them.

— When they were taking a couple, they put their children into a police orphanage; they told them they would never get their children back.

— He is in prison, and she is alone with the child, who is just beginning to talk; but she is deaf and dumb, and the child can only repeat her mumbling; so what can it learn from her; it just repeats her sounds, nothing more.

— They confiscated the medicine of a woman prisoner who was sick, and when she complained, told her they could give her rope to hang herself any time.

— One mother who works in the secret police denounced her own son; just now I made a parcel for him.

The women stop, but the sound of their voices hovers in the silence.

— Have you heard this one? The ZOMO Special Forces policeman goes to the doctor with a crowbar in his back. — Mother-in-law? asks the doctor. — No, says he, "the Uncle" (Wujek)... Mine...

The women walk away through the labyrinth, paper rustles; don't forget, take off those coloured Western wrappers, they drive the wardens mad...

Turkish Baths

The plaster is covered in small crevices left over from a bout of black smallpox some thirty years back.

With its remaining strength a crooked showcase — the lacquer cracked like lichens — hangs by one hook on the wall. Behind the misty pane three drawings by children are visible, above there's an inscription: *Always United*, first, second, third prize. Reach for the stars. In each picture the Kremlin is painted in splashes and splotches of water-colour. Out of each Kremlin, from the highest tower, a steel sputnik rears up with the air of a vicious spermatazoon that would spring an unwanted pregnancy on the world.

This is the entrance to the Turkish baths; behind it, however, could be almost any institution.

It may be that the door whose station-coloured paint is quietly peeling leads to the baths.

It may be that inside there are low corridors, slippery balustrades sweating with steam which no one touches for fear of leaving fingerprints, stairs, heavy curtains and up-right tin ashtrays. An oppressive smell of damp linen and, surely, a little woman selling admission tickets, a woman with a huge head tilting backward.

Narrow passages lead in different directions, baths, needle baths, showers, mud-baths; enamel plates with effaced inscriptions hang on the doors.

People cling to wooden benches, waiting for someone to restore their urge to live. Their eyes show deep trust as though they were preparing for confession.

Every now and again some attendants appear swathed in grey overalls and, keen-eyed, fish their customer out of the crowd.

A huge sheet bruised all over by rubber stamps divides the steam bath from a room where there is a buffet with a small table and a solitary chair, on which someone is sitting. Other figures, wrapped in lengths of towelling stand about in motionless poses, like monuments of the times, surrounded by filaments of steam as silent as first snow.

The buffet attendant's head moves behind a high counter, looking as though it is sliding along the top, which is greased with moisture. The buffet attendant clatters the bottles of Grodzisko beer. He greedily raises the bottles to his mouth as though he would like to drink from each in turn. He has a large gap between his front teeth into which he wedges the tip of the bottle-top, then jerks it from the neck at one go. He has no time to wipe away the whisks of foam that escape. The foam settles on his mouth, so that the head bobbing along the counter looks like a madman's.

He hands out the bottles, which are received in silence, tosses the coins into an old ivory plastic floor polish box, rattles the coins, then laughs at some point in space.

— Everything's fine. Halva, pumice, rubbing oil.

— All we need is whores for a knobbing — the man at the table replies. — Then we'd all be cock of the walk.

— Yes, then, halva, pumice and rubbing oil — the buffet attendant laughs through his foam-flecked lips.

— Boss. Has a dark fellow with close-cropped hair asked for me today? — the man at the table inquires.

— Not yet he hasn't — the buffet attendant gurgles. — If he was supposed to come, he'll come. Mr. Wladzio came asking, but he left.

— More's the pity. There's no fun without Mr. Wladzio. When he tells a joke, waves his prick...

— Halva, pumice and rubbing oil — roars the buffet attendant, and he wipes the tears streaming down his face on the banknote portrait of Warynski.

— Anyone got a hundred? 'Cos I'm fresh out of cash. Could do with a drink — the man at the table pushes the bottle aside.

The dumb figures in white shake their heads.

The curtain separating the room from the Turkish bath moves imperceptibly; a figure appears cautiously from behind it and, hugging the wall, flits past furtively towards the buffet.

— Hi, Attaché. How're ya.

Attaché stops abruptly in mid-step and places his bare foot warily on the tiling, as if he were testing the ground.

— H-hello.

— Let's get cracking — the man at the table winks to the dumb figures. He raises himself an inch and extracts from under his seat a book in frail, insecure covers.

— Attaché. Like to do a spot of business?

— I-I-I sh-should s-s-ay.

— Attaché, See this tome here. It's dramas. You'll net two hundred. You can have it for one, then pop down to the second-hand shop and dispose of it for two.

— I-i-i-is it w-wor-worth it?

— I should think so. It's a rarity. Listen here, Attaché. Valentyn Zielencov comes under the influence of his master Vaverlejski's Western life style. He gives priority to private affairs, and neglects production and cultural work in the theatrical ensemble attached to the factory. It is only the decisive attitude of his comrades and the educational activities of the corporate team that enable both Kostya and Valentyn to adopt a positive attitude to problems. Characteristically, all the plays have an optimistic ending, showing further evolutionary perspectives for supporters of the struggle for peace and socialism. In keeping with the historical development of humanity, the vanquished are representatives of the depraved and rotting capitalist world. The victors are splendid, high-minded people who are fighting to achieve, or have already achieved, the system of justice and happiness, communism. You can see how good the introduction is already. It's called Friends of Art. One hundred for that is an absolute gift. I wouldn't swindle you, Attaché, now would I? Would I?

— Wai-wai-wait a mo — Attaché feverishly replies, then dashes behind the curtain.

— You can open some bottles, Boss.

The buffet attendant's head glides towards a crate of bottles; he picks up several at a time like a bouquet in his two stubby hands, and the badly stuck-on labels swirl towards the floor like dried leaves.

— We've got it made here, you and me, Boss, haven't we? You cook 'em, we peck 'em. Stylish. As for that lot — he points at the silent figures in white — they ought to fix red ties to their diapers. You shouldn't let people onto the premises without red ties.

— I'll say. Halva, pumice and rubbing oil. Yes or no? The monuments in white raise their bottles to their mouths.

The curtain shudders, Attaché emerges as though he has been given a push from behind, and skulks towards the man at the table.

— Give the cash to the Boss — he nods towards the buffet attendant. Attaché halts abruptly in mid-step, then turns round and places the banknote gingerly on the counter. The buffet attendant instantly unsticks it from the moist surface.

— Take the opus — the man at the table says. Attaché grabs the book, then minces towards the curtain, but pauses again for a moment and looks imploringly at the buffet attendant.

— I-I-I say, Bo-oss, cou-ou-ouldn't I ha-a-ave a c-cou-couple of bottle-tops for the ch-ch-il-dren?

— Can't do it, ol' boy. As true as I live. I've also got to take something back to my little brood, you know.

— Ri-i-ight you a-a-are — whispers Attaché, vanishing behind the curtain with the book under his arm.

The man at the table tilts his head backwards and allows the beer to flow freely. The monuments in white adjust their towels, padding their spongy bodies in them. The steam resounds softly in white.

The door slowly opens; the newcomer stops and scans the motionless figures for some familiar faces.

— You can't be admitted in civies — comes the voice of the buffet attendant.

— It's for me, Boss — the man at the table says. — I've got to fix the lad with a job. Hi-ya.

— My buddy — the man at the table says, turning aside to the silent figures. — He was writing his Ph.D. and got kicked out at the last lap. He had the wrong sort of friends. Those types from KOR, know what I mean. Got involved in distributing those illegal rags. Now he's high and dry. *Mit Frau und Kinder.* Homeless; you ought'a help a fellow when he's high and dry, right? — he winks knowingly at his audience.

The upright figures are silent. The newcomer walks up to the table.

— Drinkie? — the seated figure asks.

— Why not?

— Boss, open us a couple of bottles. You pay the Boss, mate. Twelve a bottle.

The buffet attendant once again is foaming at the mouth, the falling bottle-tops and coins emit a delicate tinkle. The men in white drink silently.

— What sort of work are you after? — the man at the table asks.

— Well, I don't know what the prospects are...

— There are plenty of openings. For the time being you've got two options. Either the culture department at the municipal offices. Ideological work. Variety. Get me? Some sort of planning. Writing up charts and diagrams. Organizational stuff. Always something new. Or else a Scouts' broadcasting station. You can do a couple of programs for a try. Know how to use a tape recorder?

— Depends what sort.

— Outside the studio you normally take a Philips cassette. I reckon you know how to press a button. Rustle up a couple of programs, and they'll sign a contract with you. Say some sentence or other. Let's hear if you've got a broadcasting voice.

— What should I say?

— You've said it. Just what I wanted. That'll do. Your voice's OK. Now pop down to the delicatessen for a couple of bottles.

— What should I get?

— Hooch. Ordinary hooch. And something to follow. Anything will do. Piece of mortadella. Or Tshombe's ear. Or terrazzo. Anything. We must wet the deal.

— Right you are. I shan't be long. 'Cept there might be a line. But not necessarily. I'll soon be back. Things were looking bad. Couldn't find my footing. I'll be back right away. But it's sure? That job I mean?

— I should say so. Whatever did you think? So long as you like kids it's *pas de problème*, You can stop worrying.

The newcomer disappears behind the door. The silent figures in white remain motionless by their bottles.

The man sitting at the table licks a chrysanthemum of foam that has calmly blossomed on the bottleneck, pulls a cigarette out of the pack and turns towards the petrified head of the buffet attendant.

— Business is ticking over, eh? I've already knocked back a crate of hooch on that Scouts' radio station. There are more of those unemployed duffers every day. I love the Scouts for it. And you'll have your share by the by, Boss.

— I should say. Where did you net him?

— They're hanging about all over the place. He popped up in some boozer or other. You've got to put yourself in another man's shoes. Agreed?

— Halva, pumice and rubbing oil — the head of the buffet attendant laughs. And don't you throw away the beer labels. I'll take 'em home. Must bring something for the kids, you know...

Speechless, the white-clad chorus waits.

Freeze Frame Four

The wind is blowing scraps of newspaper along New World Street, the papers wipe mud off the asphalt; the patient newsprint absorbs insistent headlines like blood: production and productivity up, surplus of washing powder, economic ties with Angola expanded, Queen Marysia's quilt back in Wilanow, Polish youth active partner of the Party, White Lake white again, new activity at building sites, better and more in heavy industry, countrywomen's circles in action, communications not hit by crisis, genocide condemned, good start, new humane civilisation, softening of everyday hardship, ties of all cells strengthened, just what the people want; people are slipping along New World Street, reddish tears rolling from tightly closed lids, and on a door, a page from a school notebook, stuck on to the peeling paint with a Band-aid:

Shop closed on account of gas...

Return Visit

As you get closer and closer to that ominous structure, each step you take will be twice as heavy, and that odious front will rise to meet you, will expand and will overshadow you.

And even if you pause for a moment's respite, you are coming ever closer to the place, coated in its grey protective rot of plaster that flakes onto the pavement.

With each reluctant step it looms nearer and larger, it will engulf you and crush you. And you will look round uneasily, watching out for familiar eyes, or rather, an unfamiliar face. You will peer superstitiously over your left shoulder, casting fearful glances this way and that; just hoping that no one will see you, as that gate of all gates swallows you.

Every step will catch in your throat, climb higher and higher, increasing the distance between you and that imagined refuge where you were so patently visible in your hiding.

You will come closer and closer to that dark building.

This return visit is your reply to the callers who dropped by your place and left their card. You had given up expecting them; they were not interested that you might prefer another date or would even be happy to decline the invitation;

it occurred to you then that you and they had nothing in common.

They could not entertain the thought of your letting them down; they were looking for you quite impatiently.

You will glance back again; no one can see you, and all you will see is the everyday view behind your back: rolling life, rolling tramcars, the two-dimensional picture of people on the downgrade, a picture full of dissonances that no one will now succeed in clearing, or even try.

Passing through the gate, you will turn suddenly into the pale shadows. Humid decaying darkness will lick your face. You will be for sure the next in the procession and not the last to pay a return visit to one of these buildings. They spring up everywhere, swelling like blisters in every town, in central squares named more often than not after Liberty.

Though the button of the bell is mounted in the door-frame, you will knock on the grey wooden door; you will knock on that door which no canny bark-beetle would ever touch. You will wait an instant in silence, and then you will hear the jangle of invitation.

You will step inside and see a small corridor ending in another door mounted in a steel grating. You will see the opaque window shielding the duty-room and will set off in that direction, rummaging furiously meanwhile for your card. Emptying out your pockets.

In the duty-room, just behind the pane, you will notice an old table with its top covered in scratches, and a service cap perched at its edge. It looks for all the world as though the duty-officer's head is stuck inside it. From a distance it appears as if the duty-officer had inadvertently dropped a slice of sausage on the floor and is now kneeling behind the table and carefully trying to unstick it from the grey floorboard.

When you approach, however, you will see that the hat is empty, that there is no one in the room and no one waiting to greet you at the entrance and relieve you of your outdoor clothes. Or at least your belt and shoelaces.

For a moment you will stand undecided, but a small door inside the duty-room promptly comes to your rescue, hidden from sight by a metal cupboard. That door opens and a man emerges from behind the cupboard; he will eye you and come closer. You will think that he is no different from the others, that he has an unidentified, indecisive face devoid of capacity, just like the others. But it will be only a fleeting impression, for with a swift and seemingly shameful movement the man will reach for his hat. And when he puts it on, concealing the halo impressed on his hair, you will be looking at a totally different face. There will no longer be an unidentified man standing before you; from then on you will be standing before an official on duty.

In silence you will shove the invitation through the heart-shaped aperture in the pane; the duty-officer will glance at it, and then without looking anywhere in particular will speak for the first time as he hands you back your card.

— Floor two, room two hundred and one.

Then he will stretch his hand out towards the bell-push; you will hear the buzzer, and the door, trapped in its steel grating, will stand narrowly open before you.

You will set off upstairs, possessed by a strange sense of calm, which the gate now applauds as it slams metallically behind you. The stairs will creak beneath your tread; you will reflect that the timber has dried out; once, not that long ago, it was wet after a messy job, but now it has dried out; people will pass you by, young men clad in jeans and fashionable shirts, young men no different from their contemporaries out there; the only difference is the problems they have been given to solve, have accepted to solve; one of them turns round after you, — Mietek, drop in on me after work; you will look at him in surprise, — Pardon me, he says, and he runs off on his way. You will be passed by a couple of men in uniform and neither will give you closer scrutiny, not one of them will so much as look back at you, even though the thoughts and hearts and deeds of these people keep you company day and night.

You will climb the stairs. On the second floor you will turn to the left, and the first door you will see will bear the number two hundred and one.

You will check again to see if the number written on your invitation agrees with the number on the door, and you will knock. It opens with lightning speed, as though someone forewarned by telephone by the duty-officer had long been waiting for you there.

You hand him the invitation.

— Identity card, and wait in the corridor — says the man who opened the door.

He will take your identity card, and you will experience another moment of solitude in the dark throat of that building.

Then the door will open and you will be invited inside.

The man who took your identity card will let you in and then step towards the exit as though to surprise you from behind.

Then you will ask him.

— May I have the invitation back?

— What for?

— A souvenir.

— Not likely. We're the ones who keep souvenirs.

That sentence is uttered behind your back; you will turn round; another man in an unbuttoned white shirt will be sitting behind the desk with a smile like a bouquet of artificial flowers.

He will hold out his hand to you. Taken by surprise, you will not have the wits or prove capable of refusing. In your palm you will feel his warm fingers, not even moist, not even hard, not even.

— Please sit down.

— I'd rather stand.

— Please sit down. We'll have a little chat.

You will sit down on a chair placed this side of the desk. You will lean back, and in the protracted silence you wait for the first words.

— You're causing us a lot of trouble.

— I'm sorry.

The man will give you a searching glance, and again will say nothing for a moment.

You will observe that he often casts his eyes downwards, that he sits at an unnatural distance from the desk, and for an instant you will be intrigued. Until you realize that he has an open drawer, at the bottom of which is most likely a card with notes to help him sum you up.

— There's not a single political prisoner in the country.

— There's more.

— There's not one. That is very little. Why should there be more? That way we have peace and quiet. If need be we can always haul in a troublemaker. And talk it all over — brother, what's the point, better chuck it in and so forth. Well, but you're making a nuisance of yourself.

The man settles more comfortably in his chair, lights a cigarette, you will decline when he first holds a pack out in your direction; I don't smoke, we know you smoke, I'm not saying I never smoke; he will toss the match into a large glass ashtray on the desk, and will start peering at you again.

— I have two hours set aside for you. We can have a real heart-to-heart. Not to mince matters, as the expression goes.

— So we can.

— Now I have a couple of minor points...

— Is this to be a conversation or an interrogation?

— I'd like to have the answer to a couple of routine questions...

— In that case I presume you'll take an official statement. Right? Or am I mistaken?

The man will glance at you sadly and shake his head.

— Dear me.

Then he will be silent for a while and raise his weary gaze again.

— I had hoped... truly... Have you brought your toothbrush?

— No. I brushed my teeth this morning.

— Teeth should also be cleaned in the evening. And in the morning.

— I know. But I may answer only for the record.

The man will extinguish his cigarette and will strike his side of the desk flatly with his palm. Instantly a side door will open, and another man with the expectancy of a pointer will walk in.

— Sit down at the typewriter. You will take down the official report.

The keys begin to clatter greedily, and you will be able to sit for a moment in silence. Until the man dictates the magic words of the opening. And then you will be amazed to hear your old acquaintance ask your surname, Christian name and various other particulars he has known for a long time. And you will answer him spontaneously. — What were your activities each day of last week? Starting with Thursday? Do you know what day of the month it was?

You will nod your head without a word; the predatory hands of the man at the typewriter hang in the air, like the hands of a pianist.

— Well?

— I refuse to reply — you hear your own voice.

The face of the man behind the desk drapes itself in sadness. It will also betray the first conditioned reflex of renunciation.

For a moment he will sit with a downcast head, then without a word he will pick up the receiver delicately, like a lily, and dial a number.

— Hello, hello. It's me. Is cell number eight available? Yes? Splendid. *Ciao.*

Then he will look at you reproachfully.

— Why do you cause us so much trouble? You know how much work we have on our plates?

You will remain silent. You will lower your head and at length, with your eyes pinned on the floor, you will say lowly and sadly. — I know. And I should like to make a statement. With reference to the first question.

— A statement?

—Yes.

The man's face livens up and from somewhere under his collar a smile crawls out.

— Well, I'm all ears. If that's the case.

You will reflect for a moment, and then you will turn towards the man huddled behind the typewriter.

— I hereby testify that I am in no way involved... In no way involved, murmurs the man at the typewriter, and the greedy keys applaud you. — ... in no way involved in the explosion that took place four days ago at the foot of Lenin's statue in Nowa Huta.

You will feel the silence descend; the man at the desk will lean his head on his palm and stare aimlessly ahead.

— To hell with it... — he will say, then fall silent. You will sit quietly for a time, then you will ask apprehensively.

— Am I free now?

— Free? — the man will raise his head. — What? Free?

— May I go home now?

— You may go home.

He will slam the drawer shut in the desk and will sit up closer to the desk-top.

Without a word you will rise and hear another sentence that no longer ends in a question mark.

— And you won't sign an undertaking to keep our conversation secret...

— Frankly...I'd rather not.

He holds out his hand, but only to hand back your identity card. Then he will stick an unlit cigarette in his mouth and nod his head.

You will turn back again in the doorway. — Well, good-bye then.

— Till we meet again — you will hear him say.

You will close the door behind you. The image of the room will be blurred in the semi-darkness. You will feel yourself separated from those men by solid timber, and that shred of certainty and calm will flicker within you.

And then you will go down the creaking stairs towards the grille of the duty-room, towards the duty-officer, to-wards the rolling daylight, towards...

Freeze Frame Five

When did it happen? Could it have been in this country? When?

One can hear the tram coming on the bridge over the Vistula with a groan, looming larger in the vibrating air, suddenly slowing down; blocking its way a barbed line of soldiers, helmets shining with a sickly glow, weapons, boots which prophesy no good; the tram still moves, behind the window the driver, uneven rails shaking him like an epileptic; the tram becomes silent in stopping...

When did it happen? People being pushed out, shouting, forcing those who resist towards the greedy Black Maria. People learning in the wink of an eye to accept the role of convict; silenced heads on their shoulders, backs bent, when did it happen?

Narrow interior of the shark-like Black Maria: the student, on whom practised hands have found a pack of cards and a flute — you were going to whistle at the bosses on that pipe, you fucking son-of-a-bitch; — I wasn't going to whistle; the heavy air sniggers under the truncheons, diamonds of dust sparkle; the youngster curls up in the corner, his shoulders move in the rhythm of a tango, and the others rest, look through the confiscated cards, shuffle, cut and deal; having a moment to take a breath, one of them turns to the boy; get over here, we need one more player; so move, over here; we're playing battle; move your ass, you son-of-a-bitch...

When did it happen? Was it in this country? The well-fed Black Maria takes its load towards an unknown destination; the tear gas bites into the deserted street...

It has happened here, and now...

Topical Subject

They walked down a street so lifeless it seemed like the aftermath of an evacuation; they walked alone, or not quite alone — a stranger's footsteps loitered behind them; they were walking for his benefit too.

— Well then?

— Well, so I've stopped writing, they were saying, they also said, I was paralyzed by it all. I've no sense of distance. Chaos. Disorientation. Everything that has been so far is over and done with. Blotted out. Vanished. As they were saying. A return to those subjects implies a return to an altered self. They were explaining, I, new, now, I no longer know my own self. A state of exceptional unawareness. I've stopped writing. That unawareness is my private sin. To start writing now, they said, would be immoral. The ancients had an explanation for it. They were saying. Immoral then. Unless I attempted to write about what is going on. In this country in this time I haven't the courage to write. They wondered. I don't know if I'll ever be able to write about it. It was impossible after October. And after December. And after March. Those months are all screwed up in my mind... March was earlier... Couldn't write after June. The change in people then was not even remotely comparable to what has happened now. So it's even more difficult. There are lots of new people. New people have suddenly appeared. They were saying. People have now chosen a new nation. I'll never manage to write about that.

They walked down a street so lifeless it seemed like the aftermath of an evacuation; they walked alone, or not quite alone — a stranger's footsteps loitered behind them; they were walking for his benefit too.

One of them looked round; it was as though he had put his tired head in the warm hollow of his arm, sort of; the stranger lowered his eyes and scrutinized the paving-stones. They were cracked like earth made lifeless by drought.

It was drizzling.

In his hand the stranger held a newspaper folded in half. On one side the word freedom shone brightly in large and anxious characters, and when he seized the flapping wings of his nylon raincoat it looked as though he wanted to shield that word from the predatory locust of the wind.

— See what the newspapers write about now. Just turn round.

— Don't feel like it. I know what they write about. That's not what really matters. They wrote like that before. I used to read the stuff.

A private car emerged slowly from a side street. A doll draped in white with a huge static face was fixed to the front. A quivering eyelid kept drooping over its eye, which glittered as in a fever. The other eye was missing, presumably knocked out in some collision.

— Looks like the television news.

Garlands of yellowish, drenched tissue-paper fluttered in the rear, waving gently; the car floated in their midst like a medusa.

A woman sat inside wreathed in the same smile as the doll on the front; a man in a suit sat bolt upright and black by her side. He had an unseeing stare fixed straight ahead of him, and the corners of his mouth were turned downwards like someone whose face is paralyzed.

— How much longer are we going to write about all this? He was saying. Are no other stories ever going to materialize? That sad creep? And the laughing woman?

— His turn will come. Though as Spinoza said, usually he who laughs last has no front teeth. I don't know if that's always the case. If we don't manage to break through all that, we'll be making a revolution in prose till kingdom come.

The car stopped at the yellow light, and the pale fluttering garlands fell off into the mud like used bandages.

They turned up their collars.

— What smog.

— Bad as Kraków.

— Or Poznań.

— And that smell.

— Time for tea?

— Let's go in.

So in they went; it was cool and dark inside, and a woman was dozing behind the bar. A yellowed fringe of lace was pinned to her forehead, which bulged in a Renaissance manner. Her arm kept twitching.

— Everywhere's free. No place to sit and talk.

— How about here?

The metal stool grated against the floor tiles. The woman at the buffet raised a grudging eyelid.

— Well — she said into space. — Well. But no monkey business.

— May we?

The woman made no reply. For a moment she sat motionless on her high stool, as though she were reciting a brief prayer, then she made her descent. She was so short that she disappeared behind the bar, and the scrap of lace in her hair moving above the terrazzo counter was the only evidence of her progress.

When she came up to the table one of them ordered.

— Two teas.

She turned away.

— Does it come in bags?

— Course it does. What else do you expect?

— With lemon?

— Whatever will you think of next? — she asked with a tortured air.

The door opened and in walked the man who had been following them through the streets that day. With his newspaper he shook the tear-like drops from his nylon raincoat and fixed his stare upon the pane, beyond which the wall swelled silent with dampness.

— Shall we move? Over there by the bar?

— Right you are.

They stood up, took a few steps and sat down again.

— Let's have a fag.

— Just the thing. One always talks best out of doors.

— Got any matches?

— Somewhere.

The flame hissed in the lighter.

They raised their heads; the man in the nylon raincoat was standing at their side.

— May I give you a light? What...

They looked at him for a moment.

— I smoke too much, actually.

— I can feel something on my lungs.

They put their cigarettes aside, the clear flame subsided in the lighter. With a glassy grey gritting sound the man sat down at the table next to them.

In a clattering of glasses the woman emerged from behind the yellowish curtain that screened off the back quarters of the café. She glanced at them and stopped.

— I'll not serve that table. It's not my pad.

— Then let's move over there.

They got up and with their unlit cigarettes went after the waitress.

— Eight zlotys — she said, setting the glasses on the table.

— What, now?

— When then? So I come chasing after you later? Is that what you think?

She counted the coins and threw them into a faded pouch on her belly. When she passed by the man in the nylon raincoat, he sprang up and stood before her.

— Where's the WC here?

The woman looked up at him for the first time and promptly replied, there isn't one, low grade café — no toilet, what'll you order?

— One coffee.

— There's only lousy ersatz...

— That's OK. One small coffee.

They watched as the man crossed the room again in their direction and sat at his previous table.

— Do you take sugar?

— There isn't any.

— That's all right 'cos I don't either.

They drank a gulpful each.

The man unfolded his newspaper which hid him from sight, and next to the word freedom one of them saw another word; together they made out the name of the newspaper *Soldier of Freedom*.

— It's rotten tea.

— It hasn't brewed. Water's too cold.

—Then we might as well go.

They lit their cigarettes and stood up. They passed the waitress on their way, she was carrying a glass half-filled with yellowish coffee. They glanced once more at the café tables, the bar with its sepulchral terrazzo counter, then went out into the street.

— Let's wait a minute, OK?

— And finish our fags.

They stood in silence, circled by humid swollen smoke. Overhead, grey pigeons careered about in the air. They watched.

Then one of them threw his cigarette-end onto the road-way; one of the pigeons fluttered down and tried to grip the smouldering butt in its beak, but failed to fly away before a speeding car — the damp air gave its wings no support.

They heard the mudguard strike the bird in flight, there was a whirl of feathers; the car was gone.

The pigeon lay in the street; its wings, helplessly out-spread, took up really very little space.

— Look. The other one's fucking it.

They saw another pigeon, its feathers bristling, clinging to the spine of the dead bird.

Another car sped past. The displaced air jerked the be-wildered male, but it did not relinquish its prey.

— Eerie.

They exchanged looks.

— Eerie. What now? Shall it be mine, for me to write about?

— Why yours? We both saw it together.

— Shall we toss for it?

— Or we'll both write. We'll write it together. It's an OK topic. Pity to miss it.

From behind their backs they heard the sound of softly closing doors. The man in the nylon raincoat appeared. In his hand he held the folded newspaper. From one side the word soldier loomed black in large and anxious characters.

— Well? We can go now — one of them said.

— So we can — replied the other.

…along the lifeless street…

Freeze Frame Six

The woman struggles with the phone booth door, shouting into the receiver, — I can't travel to see Mother tomorrow, I am busy for the next two days, and I've got to see the doctor as well...

She stops suddenly, bewildered, as a stranger's voice interrupts firmly — I remind you that you must speak clearly, using simple sentences only.

The woman rushes out, stops, moves again, and then the dark entrance of the church draws her in. She slumps onto a bench, drowned in the waxy silence, and only then, quickly, superstitiously, crosses herself; she sits for a long time, waiting.

People pray silently in the side aisle by the Easter Tomb; a helpless body of Christ on a prison bed, and by him, on a bundle of straw, white paper hearts like snow; children have written the best of their Easter good deeds: I gave up my seat in the tram, I got a good mark at school, I helped a blind man cross the road, I washed the dishes for my mum, I am not using naughty words any more, I gave up my seat on the bus, I've given up lying for good, I stood in line at the butcher's instead of my mother, I promise to work harder at school, I'll look after my little brother, I helped an old lady fetch coal from the cellar, I gave up my seat to a sick man, I shared my orange with a schoolmate...

Shabby Lodgings

To reach the radio you must first decide that you wish to do so, then take your time mustering the strength, then finally force your reluctant hand to the task.

You slowly advance your palm from the warm space that has collected by your side, cautiously expose your fingers beyond the confines of the bedcover, and instantly feel teeming mites of cold assail you.

Your palm wanders ever further from you, then ceases to be yours; of its own accord it moves towards the receiver, rests briefly on the protruding knobs.

Finally your index finger performs the essential act; your hand returns with relief to its former position, back to sleep in the nest.

The radio picks up the second program only. In the beginning there is a long silence, so penetrating that you become convinced the radio will not speak to you this time.

Then a magic eye begins to glow greenly through its receding hood.

Voices begin laboriously to force their way through the coarse, dust-choked material covering the speaker. They are distant, but can be heard with increasing distinctness. It is a music program for children and the producer first gives the theme by tapping out a melody on a piano. Then all repeat the first stanza mechanically and discordantly like so many broken tin toys. The low and resolute tone of the compère makes itself heard above the voices.

The damp air slides down from the windowsill; you try to cover yourself with the skimpy child's coverlet which you found in this rented bed, and you hear the words of the song emerging with difficulty from the speaker.

The sunlight shines through all the sky,
Through all our land so fair,
Our land demands your loyalty,
You are her own true heir.

The frail voices of the children repeat the words with diffidence, gusts of wind flare the curtain, even though the window has not been opened since autumn. Scraps of cotton wool stuffed into the cracks have long since gone grey and now look like sputum.

The sunlight shines through all the sky, through all our land so fair, comes the male solo. A noise is heard outside the high door, pimpled with paint, then footsteps. They stop in the corridor; you hear someone listening; then the hook of the door handle jerks and the door opens to a singsong of hinges; that forty-year-old woman appears in the yellowish rectangle of the door frame.

— Well, yes — she says and breaks off, or else her thought deserts her; she walks over to the stove, opens the door and begins to rattle the poker against the protruding ribs of the grate.

She has her back turned, and when she stoops to peer into the cold cavity, you see the puckered hollow between her thigh and her calf that is like the clenched and toothless mouth of an old woman, exposed by her hitched-up dressing gown.

— Perhaps I should call the doctor from the welfare center...or what...

You make no reply so as not to squander those chilled words that would explain nothing, but twice over you succeed in executing a motion of the head; it is meant to signify negation, and the woman interprets your motion correctly; so she just shrugs her shoulders helplessly.

— At work they don't accept that sort of illness without a doctor's certificate, you must have your L4 form.

— I won't go back to that job — you are suddenly amazed to hear your voice; she looks up at you.

— Everyone has to work.

— That's exactly what I'm saying — you hear the reply.

She leaves the room without closing the door behind her; you can see the pregnant darkness of the corridor into which the tinny words of the song now roll, gracelessly, but sounding with greater impact:

The sunlight shines through all the sky,
Through all our land so fair,
Our land demands your loyalty,
You are her own true heir.

The song is lost in the fetid darkness; again you hear footsteps, and the darkness suddenly lights up and glows as though a blazing hoop was rolling over the parquet.

The woman appears carrying a monstrance in her outstretched hand: glimmers of coal scooped a moment ago out of her stove wink and twitch on a tin spade.

She enters the room; the rattling coals vanish inside the stove and stop chattering. Stifled by the cold air, they subside. She puts the shovel aside, slams the door and fastens it tight. Then, turning away, with one hand she gathers up the dressing gown over her loose breasts and strokes the icy tiles voluptuously with the other.

— Soon it will be nice and warm.

— Very good — you hear a man's voice. -- And now I should like to hear the first two lines of the second stanza.

For every day our land's more lovely,

Red and white roses everywhere...

The thin voice of a child rings soullessly.

— How about tea — the woman says.

You look at the stove tiles, which are dull as formica, yes, if you could, not a bad idea, you reply.

Her hair is tied behind with a cool violet ribbon. You half close your eyes to avoid looking at the wedding portrait which hangs above the pallet; a black and white picture with only the mouths of the couple outlined in vampire red; withered smiles cringe between the gleaming teeth.

The keyboard in the speaker bangs out the tune, then the bedraggled chorus breaks out.

For every day our land's more lovely,

Red and white roses everywhere...

You raise your eyelids; the woman sets a bleary glass on the chair, puts a newspaper on the bedcover and sits down next to it.

— It's today's — she says.

— I'll wait till it cools. To wash down the powder. It won't go down otherwise.

— Sleeping powders are dangerous.

— They don't even help me to sleep.

She bends over and brutally switches off the radio. Her eyes roam along the dusty corners of the room in search of some stray thought. Then she draws a spray of air into her lungs; her breasts wander upwards, downwards, shaping the first letter of the alphabet in a shadow on the wall.

You know she is about to speak.

— And yesterday I lined up for seven hours for herring at the deli corner, and some old geezer couldn't take it and snuffed it, and the ambulance came but he was dead as a nail. Well, so they wouldn't take him away as they haven't got a cold-store, so they said to call for a van. Somebody covered his face over with *The People's Tribune* and he lay there just like the First Secretary. I won't be able to eat those herrings now.

You grasp the newspaper and set up a barricade of lacy newsprint.

— May I see?

— Frankly it's better out loud — she says. -- For what it's worth I can always read it myself. Except that the first and second page were on television yesterday. About anti-socialist elements.

— Then what about the centre page? — you ask with some effort.

— Ah. There's an interview with Ryszard Gontarz. Who on earth is Ryszard Gontarz...aha, here we are, ...*publicist and playwright.*

— You see.

—*...And playwright. Some time ago I saw a splendid show at the Warsaw Citadel commemorating the anniversary of Felix Dzierzynski's birth. You are the author of the scenario. How is it that when your writing to date has dealt only with contemporary problems you should now turn to a historical subject? The question was put by Anna Klodzinska. Now for the answer. In the public view Felix Dzierzynski is a figure cast in steel, who never wavered or yielded to any human frailty. I wanted to depict him not just on the grand scale but as an extremely sensitive man, impressionable and romantic. Hence the title,* Romantic Revolutionary.

She hides herself from your eyes with the newspaper screen. Outside the window the light is already dispersing, the day is on the ebb. You cannot see her, but you can feel her leaning, resting on her elbow; her breast slouches against your foot and lends it some warmth.

— Let's try something else — the woman whispers. — How about a poem? Here's a poem. *Poets' corner: Bohdan Chorazuk.* The words rattle softly like chick-peas.

We have a mine of gold at hand
The ideal aggregate
Of Politburo members
And honest workers' sweat

— ... no, it won't do ... — she says shamefacedly. She puts aside the cool pages, she is silent; the heat of her fingers radiates up your knee.

—Here's a travel article. *Stand beneath the Eiffel Tower on Panorama Street. Coloured photographs against a background of the Eiffel Tower, the Arc de Triomphe or the Egyptian pyramids without leaving the homeland may be ordered at the new shop shortly to open by the Polifoto Cooperative in Panorama Street. Lifelike scenery and proper posing will give your photos that authentic look. To allow for full preparation of background and model, the entire process will last about half an hour...*

She stops reading, remaining screened; you stretch out your hand. For a moment it wanders among pockets of air and then chances on a shape. You press and again you hear the muffled voices.

And through our homeland far and wide
The youthful fires are burning there.

Her hand proceeds higher and even higher; you hear the rustle of her motion; the woman leans her head on your knees and you feel the desperate pulsing of the artery in the hollow of her neck; she says something in a hasty, lustreless voice that fades away.

You are at a distance, watching, your eyes rake your body in unastonished scrutiny.

Footsteps can be heard outside the window; the woman straightens up without withdrawing her hand. — It's my old man back from work, she says, I recognize his step.

She rises slowly and pushes your glass towards you with a gesture full of weariness. You see the cool violet ribbon that binds her hair.

The door closes with a soft heave, and then as through a fog you hear the two metallic clinks of a lock being opened.

You raise yourself on your elbow and peel the cellophane shell from the sleeping powder. You place it in your mouth and wash it down with watery tea.

From the corridor voices are heard balancing as on a tightrope, then everything falls silent and the flurried woman slips through the chink between darkness and light, two gentlemen have come from the Committee and say they want to know why you've been away from work for the last four days and whether you're ill; and they want to see you, they're waiting out there.

You sit up on the bed, the coverlet falls away from your chest, but breathing's none the easier for that.

— Well then ...that means...they can't come... I refuse to see them. Kindly tell them that I haven't been to work for four days because I've spent the last four days eating my little red book page by page, each contribution stamp, every seal, my surname, photograph, and that the worst of the lot was the cover, because it was so hard, but I chewed it very thoroughly and now it will take me to the end of my life to digest it and I'll never fully digest it... neither the covers nor the colour nor my own name which I've swallowed. So I have all that to digest, and I shall no longer have time to go to work. Well, and tell them to get along without me and go back where they came from. There's no question of their coming in here...'*Raus*...

— Am I to repeat your exact words? — she asks in alarm.

— My exact words.

She turns slowly away and you hear her whispering, she repeats the words so as not to get them wrong, he hasn't been to work because he's spent the last four days eating his little red book page by page every contribution stamp every official seal his surname photograph, well but the worst of the lot was the cover, because it was so hard, but he chewed very thoroughly and now it will take him until the end of his life to digest it though he'll never fully digest the covers or the... , she screens you from the darkness with the leaf of the door. You turn up the radio which receives only the second program and you wrap yourself in the child's coverlet.

— And now the whole stanza. Nicely now.

Beads of dust flicker round the box, a voice spills from the speaker.

For every day our land's more lovely,
Red and white roses everywhere,
And through our homeland far and wide,
The youthful fires are burning there.

You feel you are falling; you feel how the sputter of sleep muddies your thoughts for the first time after your own hundred days; you are falling, becoming brittle, the thud of your dry heart turns cold; you are falling...

Freeze Frame Seven

Planes that take off from this airport for the metropolis of the East sometimes land on the other side of the world, in West Berlin.

These few subdued people will soon board a plane, which they will hijack to Frankfurt; they will stay nearby, waiting for an onward flight, and until the moment of their irrevocable landing on American soil, none of them will call himself an *émigré*.

More than one empty bottle of Russian vodka will fly out the window of an expensive boarding house as they wait.

— A pal of mine phoned yesterday, asking me not to forget to bring a bag of 20-zloty coins because they fit the vending machines over there in place of 5 or 2-mark pieces; he said they've already run out of Polish money. He must be crazy, but I heard his voice quite clearly.

The check-in will soon be finished and the tired air hostess can hardly look at the passenger talking to her; later she will recognize his face from Kodacolor prints.

These people, soon to be hijacked, pretend to be calm; in their sweaty fingers they clutch these strange, brand-new passports...

Journey

The elevator door closed suddenly like a mouth in mid-speech; he was alone inside with that shred of a woman teetering on a dilapidated crimson stool. She seemed asleep, leaning her head against the cool wall of the cabin; he was silent, pervaded by a sense of calm.

The woman dozed, eyes fixing on him through a blurred gaze. Her half-open lids quivered like acacia petals.

That sense of calm did not elicit any surprise in him; he had expected it and had been waiting for its gentle wave ever since the moment he had first thought of the palace. Once when he came out of the station, he had raised his eyes and seen that pile looming out of the fog of early dawn; it looked as though a mischievous Stalin had shat in the middle of the gigantic square; he had then recalled that a ride to the top cost only a few zlotys.

Now he was standing in this small cage and felt pervaded by a sense of calm.

The hand of the sleepy woman rose grudgingly towards the lever, his feet began to feel the pressure of the floor; he raised his head and saw figures lighting up one after the other, one floor after the other, in the grey squares above the door.

He held his hand in his pocket and with his fingers touched the oval disc the cloakroom attendant had given him down below when he handed in his jacket; I don't need a check, he said to the one-armed man as he placed his jacket on the marble slab, what do you mean, really, the one-armed man looked at him; how can I give you back your coat, I mean really; he vanished for a moment behind a screen of lifeless transpiring garments, then threw him the token; it rolled along the slippery stone and fell rattling to the floor. He did not want to prolong the conversation. He was waiting patiently for the peace that would shortly descend. He swiftly bent down to pick it up and stuffed it in his pocket. Now he felt it with his fingers.

— How long've you been working this thing? — he said to the woman who quivered at her post like a black spider in a bath of boiling water.

— How long you say? — she said to herself, unable to understand the question. — How long. Time out of mind. All me life. Time out of mind.

— And you don't get bored.

— Bored you say. Work's varied. First 'un goes up. Then 'un goes down. Sometimes 'un goes to the thirty-second. Other times 'un goes to the eleventh. Varies...

His feet felt the uniform pressure of the elevator floor.

He remained silent, kept peering at the checkerboard of floor numbers. With each successive flash he climbed higher, further, closer.

— And anyway four years ago on Women's Day they gave a bonus, not to be claimed back, two hundred zlotys.

But there's no justice. That bitch on the second shift got two hundred and thirty. There's no justice — the woman suddenly uttered into the void. Then she raised to him her eyes, rabbit-like from lack of sleep and lined with little red veins, and for a moment he saw despair and hatred in those eyes; then they were again hooded by the lids.

Thoughts had ceased to pain him. His fingers now sought out the oblong card in the recess of his pocket; it was the return ticket he had had to buy down at ground level.

— A ticket up to the terrace. One way please.

— One way only — how on earth — the ticket-man looked at him, and his arm kept making convulsive movements as though he were trying to block his ear. Are you going to return from the sights up there by the stairs? That big world?

— Yes. One way only please.

— There ain't no one-way tickets. There's only return tickets. You can get one-way tickets on the tram if you fancy. But not for our sightseeing here. But you can on the tram — he said rumbling with spasmodic laughter. He took a long time to calm down as he stroked his cheek with his arm.

His fingers now began to crumple the ticket, crush it, shred it. They moved of their own accord, without his being aware.

The walls of the elevator were scribbled over with dates, initials, place names, I was here, in this elevator I lost my cherry to Lis, We the Union of Polish Youth are unafraid, Gomulka is a big little prick — school teacher from Nysa, Krakow men are pricks not Poles, Babiuch has bedroom eyes, You can keep your student mag — give us back *Plain Speech*, better Kania than Vanya, I love Marycha Robaszkiewicz, the queen of Kozalin, Scoutmaster's gone — fucking's on, Danka — quit fooling before they start screwing, Grabbed meat, filched bread, guess his name — it's our Ed, Confederation of Independent Poland are runts. Some words were written in ball point, others scratched with sharp implements.

— When do they do it? — he asked, running his nail along the crooked contour of an engraved heart.

— Can't stop 'em. When you're catnapping straightaway they pull out some nail and they're at it again. The worst is when they're against the system because then they pick on me. Yes, as if it was my fault the system's the way it is. Can't stop 'em. There's no one doesn't want to leave his mark as a memento-like.

— I don't.

— You do-o-o-nt? — she broke out into a voiceless laugh. 'Cos I'm watching your hands. Everyone does. But when they comes and picks on me I put the blame on that bitch from the second shift. Four years ago on Women's Day they gave two hundred zlotys unreclaimable bonus. But there's no justice. The bitch on the second shift got two hundred and thirty...

His feet felt the pressure from the elevator floor imperceptibly diminish. Already he was high and close. The shaggy palm of the woman wandered towards the lever.

He raised his eyes. His last box with the floor number lit up sympathetically, and that was it.

— There then — said the woman.

— Have you ever been on the terrace?

For a moment her astonished lids revealed two eyes streaked like marble balls.

— Why the blummin' hell should I? There's a howling gale up there, somethin' awful. What, to get me head blown off?

— Don't ask me. To see the view...

— I'm all right where I is. In the warm. But there's no justice.

The door wheezed open.

The dim light-bulb gave way to the day.

He felt an increasing sense of relief, a volatile lightness, but he turned his head back again to look at the necrotic woman.

She remained silent and motionless.

He withdrew his gaze and went on his way.

He passed the bend in the lofty corridor. And then the daylight hit him.

Space unexpectedly made itself felt.

He was not looking; he could not see the greedy clouds of fog crowding in, he could not hear the muffled echoes from below.

He moved forward then stopped. His eyelids were lowered. He was expecting nothing.

The terrace was empty, tousled by gusts of rain. He took a few light steps and forgot about everything once and for all. Only his feet sensed the diligent unbroken pulse of the ground.

He felt the impact of stone — the humid barrier held him up for another brief moment.

Then he opened his eyes again.

The terrace was immense. It was not situated on the highest storey, and the roof above it was supported by heavy concrete pillars.

After he had looked more carefully he realized that a shiny impassable steel netting was spread out tightly between the columns, the barrier and the roof. He noticed the clear translucent gleams of liquid fog on the metal.

He stood rooted to the spot and stared at the steel netting.

A low cloud rode up, clasped him in a clammy white stillness but could not lift him into space. The steel netting made that impossible. He stood immersed in the cloud and painfully recollected everything....

Freeze Frame Eight

The psychiatrist is pouring vodka down his throat without blinking an eye and is talking, his hair greying to the right, asymmetrically.

— I am giving in my notice, I am changing my profession.

The glass in front of him is full again, a crystal-like drop bursting on its rim. — As a doctor I cannot help anybody anymore, that makes me grey on the right side, asymmetrically; a patient tells me, I am under surveillance, nowhere can I be alone, they are everywhere; they put a bug in my home and as if that was not enough, they listen in to my telephone conversations, so I stopped making calls, they even open my letters, even postcards they read, everything, and when I go out into the street, they want to poison me with gas; simply, they want to gas me; they are everywhere; and the right side of my hair is getting greyer from it and I wish to reply to him, that I also have the same symptoms, exactly the same, that it is only a harmless persecution mania which will pass, that it is easy to cure and he should not bother about it too much; both of us would be cured of this mania; yesterday I was on duty in the emergency ward and I was taken to an unsuccessful suicide case, it was an activist, he had been in hiding for months and his nerves could take no more; he cut minor veins, but I knew that tomorrow, or the day after tomorrow, he would do it for real; inescapable, and from the ambulance, by the radiophone, I contacted the police and I reported it, because prison, that is his only rescue and therapy; they said they are on their way to get him and thanked me, and at that moment I understood that this was my last day working in this profession. — He is pouring vodka down his throat without blinking an eye, placing the chilled glass against his hair...

No Sound of Footsteps in the Treetops

A deserted square with a naked tree in its midst, standing dead still because sham gusts of wind can take no grip on its scant branches.

The sky above the square is ashen and congealed in space as though an extinct part of our planet were mirrored in it.

A row of posts kept in spotlight from dusk to sluggish dawn; a row of posts in a hoar-frost of light, each decked in a crown of thorns, a steel girdle with sharp spikes pointing downwards, secured at the height of upraised arms; if any prisoner in a fit of madness wanted to climb above the flat roofs, those spikes would come to meet him.

Rows of barracks; iron bars gleam inanely in the windows; barracks are everywhere, at all the corners of this moderately-sized universe. They are separated from the square by a high netting crowned with barbed wire.

The square is deserted; not long ago people wandered along the small loop of pathway; a mist of exhalation and stillness rose gradually above them, boots kicked up a dust of snow. Timorous minutes of the allotted stroll slipped past.

There were twenty of them, perhaps thirty. Several cells.

The guards who followed them with hate-filled eyes cowered in the sharp air; one of them hid behind the metal netting; it gave him a spot of shelter without obscuring the view.

The men wandered in file and in silence. Boots kicked up a dust of snow, brief minutes for walking slipped swiftly away.

They had turned up here for war to be waged in peace.

For war to break out on a grim December day, enemies had to be identified. For doing battle, the last battle for so many years, an enemy army had to be found.

Those and those too were called the enemy. They were made prisoners before being told that war had broken out. Prisoners were taken first in this war, and war was declared afterwards. Before the tanks began to roll through the squares, the prisoners were already behind walls, surveyed by towers bristling with guards.

Before the battle the prisoners were taken.

Those who until recently had been roving loose on a tightly watched rein were invented, so the war could go on.

The dead and the missing were also designated for that war. The dead and the missing were not invented. Their crosses are real, as real as the crosses of the brave.

A deserted square and a naked tree. Another few frail minutes will fall away, and the guards will escort the next group out. Then they will cower in the sharp air, and one of them will hide behind the metal netting which will give him a spot of shelter without obscuring the view.

The prisoners will wander in silence. A woman will suddenly wake up in a faraway house. A guard will peer around suspiciously.

The war goes on; beyond the wall the forest returns to life in the ascending light, but there is no sound of footsteps in the treetops.

Freeze Frame Nine

Patches of steel-coloured paint on the cold walls of the houses cover the slogans of an earlier time.

People sneak out at night with buckets of bright paint to liquidate those grey patches of bad conscience, a constant reminder of the slogans underneath.

With quick brush strokes they paint some crooked houses, hang yellow suns above them, and fill the freshly drawn path with shapeless, small-headed human figures.

So by the time the morning painfully awakes, everything looks as if unseen gangs of unruly children have decorated the walls of their beloved town.

A man is spat out of the bus, his empty gaze arrested for a moment by the picture of a cheerful gnome; he shakes himself, wipes his forehead, and with this careless movement knocks off his beret, which is too big for his head. Taking it up from the dust, he seems to genuflect to a passer-by whom he suddenly grabs by the sleeve, and into whose eyes he gazes beseechingly.

— Please, Sir. Which way to the United States, Sir?

— Oh...er...first to the right, then straight on. Let go of my sleeve. Yes, it's somewhere there, turn left and then straight on.

— Which way? I'm not with you.
— Oh, come off it...

White Night

It is a frosty day; an acrid frost crushes the thorny spikes in the air.

It is a bleak, hard, Muscovite December day.

The day is self-evident, but the man stops suddenly amid the snowflakes and simply cannot believe; how is it possible, he repeats, how is it possible; the edge of his upraised collar freezes against his cheek, it is impossible, another war; a gust of wind parts the white curtain from behind which the bus stop, like an aquarium, looms into sight; a bunch of lonely people stare at him; how is it possible, another war; what shall I tell the family, what shall I give them to eat, another war, and I haven't got a good *Kennkarte**...another...

People stare at him; a storm of white flakes swirls impatiently above his head. They shift their weight from one leg to the other in search of warmth; behind their backs the glass wall quivers and rings. On it a harsh sentence has been bill-posted: the proclamation of martial law. A relentless hand has crossed through those words and substituted the Nazi formula — *Bekanntmachung*.

* *Kennkarte.* The special identity card issued to Poles during the Nazi occupation in World War Two.

Other words and phrases are scrawled, on the glass wall of the aquarium, as though in a duel: TV lies; Polish People's Republic=Leonid's private ranch; KOR=Jews; We demand the registration of Solidarity without changes in the Statute; We'll avenge Katyn; the Economic Aid Council gives everything to Russia and shit to Poland; KOR=Bonn spies. Another sentiment on the side wall expands with every hour; initially only a few black words: *The eagle will not be vanquished by the crow.* Then further revisions are made: *the crow will croak before the eagle's vanquished, the fucking crow will croak before the eagle's vanquished, the fucking croaking crow will blow before...*

One must be cautious, very cautious, the man repeats, one must be cautious, there could be a round-up any minute, any minute...it's no laughing matter...there's a war on...

People stare at him; war, war, someone mutters, we know it's war; sooner or later there had to be war, I mean how long could they be expected to wait, bloomin' red spiders; thirty years ago they issued us an ultimatum, yes or no, head or tails, you can't have it both ways, communism and belt up, or else war — the choice is yours...so then it's war...

— But to do it to your own people, your *own* people, for a Pole to declare war against Poles...I mean ...a woman whispers through whitened lips.

— Poles my ass, you'd first have to sew collars onto their Russian peasant shirts to make them look like Poles, the motherfuckers. Real Polish army collars.

— What sort of people are they...what sort of people can they be...yet they say the father of one of the top brass died in Katyn...incredible...for a son to fall so low.

— Died in Katyn... He didn't die, he killed himself. Got drunk and fell off a watch tower. You'd better listen properly if you're going to listen at all...

— There could be massacres, the solitary man speaks up; there could always be massacres; a gust of wind presses his words into a bend in the wall.

— He's standing out there in the cold — someone from the aquarium says. — He'll freeze to death in that frost. Hey mister. Come under the roof, come under the shelter.

His mouth moves, but the words cannot pass through the numb glass; mister, come under the roof, it's warmer here, someone repeats tapping his finger against the pane; transfixed with sounds the man suddenly doubles up from cold, is screened for a moment by a shutter of wind and snow; an instant later the air clears again, but the man has gone; he has been swallowed up by a protective gateway.

The people in the aquarium tread down the snow with their feet.

— The spring will be ours — someone says. — I saw it written, the soldiers were rubbing the words off a tank, the winter's yours, the spring is ours, some kid painted it on, they were rubbing it off. The spring will be ours...so they say...

The words freeze to the glass, snowflakes twirl in a cradle of wind, a young woman's face comes alive inside her collar.

— You are cold — says someone in a crimson plastic coat that creaks with every word. — They hijacked that bus to Sweden, didn't they? Feeling cold?

— Freezing.

— You'd soon warm up again...if a real man cuddled you — says the man, and he starts to shake with ribald laughter; the crimson armour creaks in the snow.

— The real men are in prison now — the woman replies, and the crimson plastic goes still.

Then out of the silence a bus suddenly emerges. The red smudge grows bigger, and the motionless crowd returns with difficulty to life, as in the moment after awakening.

— We've waited an hour and forty minutes.

— We're lucky it's here... It might not have come at all...with the war...

The bus proceeds without speed or sound; its wide windscreen is frozen over. The driver presses his white brow against the pane and studies the road ahead.

Then the front doors open like an accordion, but the little crowd of people in the aquarium is again rooted to the ground. A man appears on the step followed by a young boy. They look like father and son. It looks as though the son is leaning on his father, and the father leading his son. The man pulls the boy after him; the boy's hand repeats every movement of the man's hand. A moment later they are standing in a lather of snow. Within the frame of the door the blurred faces look like part of a group portrait. The man stoops again, and with his free hand picks up some white papers from the step of the bus which he hurriedly stuffs into his pocket; one flies out of his fingers and falls breathless at the feet of the waiting crowd.

Leaflets ... someone says in a whisper, he was distributing leaflets; the boy plods after the man. Their hands tense up and one can see now that they are joined by handcuffs.

Those waiting watch in silence. Then the young woman speaks in a stifled voice, speaks with difficulty — do something, do something, do...

The image of the man and the boy is softened by the innocent whiteness; a blister of warm steam swells in the open door of the bus; the people huddle inside without looking back; submissively they do not turn back, but retreat into the comfy interior. The young woman remains alone at the bus stop with her head downcast; the man and the boy have vanished.

The doors close, bursting the bubble of warmth; the bus drifts away.

The woman stands stock-still. A leaflet lies at her feet, but she cannot bend to pick it up; she can no longer move.

Freeze Frame Ten

This town's Victory Square has lost its last battle; now it is only a fragment of space, closed in by a high hermetic fence; some time ago people were laying flowers here, creating a flower cross in memory of the dead, those killed by a treacherous assassin. Now the only symbol is the dead Hotel Victoria, in front of which the tout quickly tries to get rid of his zlotys, buying dollars or other hard currency; he whispers into the emptiness and looks at the solitary tart; a secret policeman attempts to get her. — Do you think you can screw me because of your badge, you idiot?

A bit further on, under the weathered statue of Victory whose sword has wasted away, a bus stops, and through the dirty front window one can see the guide. His lips move silently, forcing some words down the microphone; behind the glass, people, motionless like crabs, some of them in sullied sleep, others mindlessly stare ahead...

Day of Mist and Cloud

It is morning, but the wartime day cannot emerge from half-darkness.

The tumid air subsides heavily and the snow alone emits a kind of low gleam. People's faces are plunged in shadow.

The innocent white of the crossroads is scarred by the caterpillar-tracks of tanks. They have rolled past many times in the night, sowing alarm more than usual, boring their way through the city. In two days it will be Christmas.

One of the tanks has come to a dead halt at the crossroads — broken down or abandoned by its crew, no one can tell.

There is a bitter frost. A metal basket full of throbbing coals stands by the wall of a house whose inmates do not come near the windows. Several soldiers stoop over the brazier, stretching their hands toward it like beggars; the green flames pulse between their fingers.

Others helplessly surround a car they have just stopped; the NCO peers greedily inside, then in the back he discovers a fuel can, an object banned for several days now; he pulls it out and opens it, and a yellow stream trickles along the curb; the driver turns his head aside and does not look.

The car drives off, stillness descends, withdrawn passers-by flounder in silence; a mud-coloured police van, we call it a disco, lies in ambush by the tank. It has not yet grabbed its fill today.

The militiamen prowl the neighbourhood, leer insolently into faces, check papers, rummage through handbags. Sometimes they lead someone towards the van, and then the eyes of the onlookers come back to life, filled with curiosity and fear.

Two uniformed men stand facing the wall with arms upraised, as though they are about to be shot on the instant, ineffectually trying to paint over an inscription that sprouted during the night. Two words persistently rise to the paint's surface: *Cunta Junta.*

The soldiers gathered at the rhythmic fire suddenly turn round; a woman has come up to them. They peer at her grey coat, at the ashes of hair tumbling onto her shoulders from under a black headscarf; there is confusion in their eyes; she speaks to them slowly, fervently; they avoid her gaze, they are silent; any moment now the NCO will appear with several militiamen; they lead the old woman away, and she offers no resistance.

The soldiers hang their heads lower still, but the brazier throws intense heat and light on their foreheads and they have nowhere to hide; the automatic pistols hanging at their belts knock against their sides, rub painfully, excruciatingly.

The face of a man about to be swallowed up by the voracious police van is white as snow; the Christmas tree he was gingerly carrying has been knocked out of his arm; it is now being looked over, evaluated, assessed with a proprietary eye by a corporal. Then it is raised from the ground, shaken free of white dust and set up in a secluded corner. The corporal will guard it, it will be his.

At the bus stop people are huddled in a crowd; they look grey in the glassy milk-like fog, they are waiting...

— It was different during the occupation, it was... The Germans used to kill us, but they let us get on with life...

— I tell you. Before the war there was a great hue and cry, Jews to Madagascar, Jews to Madagascar. We're the ones that ought've buggered off there. I mean it.

There is suddenly some traffic at the crossroads, the air vibrates, a minibus draws up to the curb. A cameraman leaps out, then an officer; they help a woman, opulent sheepskin, a carmine foam of smile on her lips, to extricate herself from the snug interior; someone obligingly offers her his arm, the cameraman selects a spot; with a snigger she slumps down finally in the wool-like snow.

In her fingers she grips several red carnations, which are shrivelled by the frost in an instant, and a gramophone record in a coloured sleeve.

She now poses in the shadow of the motorcar, waiting; words spill quietly from her mouth like beads: — We Polish women and Polish mothers,...we owe it to *you* that peace has prevailed in the streets of our towns and in our homes...civil war...and the villages, you have prevented...you have... counter-revolution...we shan't renounce the achievements of socialism...

The soldiers assembled over the meagre source of fire also stand still, their outstretched palms stung by the fateful, opaline sparks; two officers stride towards them, the cameraman makes himself comfortable.

The officers spot out the tallest among them, give him a good looking over; —How's service? one of them asks. — Yes Sir, the soldier draws to attention.

— As you know Christmas will soon be with us. You lads have been selected to receive a gift and a modest soldier's, you know, posy of flowers, from the hands of our representative of Polish motherhood; seeing as you perform your duty, you know, in exemplary fashion and carry out the assignments with which you are entrusted, you will have the honour of being immortalized by Polish television and shown to the general public on the silver screen; are you ready? The citizeness representing Polish motherhood is waiting, truth, women's organizations. Stand tall, soldier.

And the soldier takes one step back, he wants to say something, but no one is listening to him, so he stands motionless as in a dream; there is bustle around him, the camera hisses venomously; his colleagues draw warily aside to avoid that eye; the soldier sees before him the smudge of face grinning vapidly, on account of Christmas we Polish women and Polish mothers...we owe it to you that peace has prevailed in the streets of our towns and in our homes civil war and the villages...you have prevented... you have...counter revolution...we shan't renounce the achievements of socialism...

The soldier thinks frantically, no answer comes into his head; he can now see the woman's broad back and mechanically repeats behind her, at the colonel's orders we launched a spontaneous collection on behalf of the flood victims...

There is no more camera or microphone; the minibus moves off; through its window the bunch of red carnations scattered on the seat can be seen; the soldier lowers his head and finds that he is holding a record in a coloured sleeve; but they've made an ass of you, someone says from the sidelines; he tosses the record on the seething ants' nest of coal; a mute black smudge spills out...

The tank at the crossroads returns suddenly to life; the engine gasps for breath, and the armour-plating begins to quiver delicately; the tumid air subsides heavily...

Freeze Frame Eleven

The small deserted square has become a true bazaar and the woman, wrapped in a cocoon of rags, huddles alone — a handful of wilted carrots scattered at the feet of politicians on the front page of a newspaper; are the carrots good enough for children, somebody asks timidly; sweet as honey, comes the emphatic reply, sweet as honey.

— How fresh is the cabbage?

— Fresh as we are.

— Lovely eggs, tiny ones, nice!

— Or else I'll hang myself on that belt maybe -- says a man with a coarse laugh, having nothing more to sell.

One vendor has displayed bright cookbooks on his stall, full of forgotten notions and aromas, and nearby in a shop called The House of Shoes a man, staring avidly into the lifeless face of the salesclerk, shows her his coupon.

— I fell down coming from work. And when I was nearly home, I almost slipped again. Most probably because my shoes are worn out. So I ask you, what am I supposed to walk around in?

— Oh, go away, sir — the salesclerk stirs in her lethargy — do go away...

Bitter Red Star

For two days now they had been sitting face to face; the wind had driven in an early dusk and the bulb glowed shamelessly; they sat face to face, divided only by the yellowish desk.

He sat with his back to the unprotected wall, behind his back the plain-clothes man had a metal cupboard; the light glimmered faintly on its polished door.

They had been sitting face to face for two days now, the plain-clothes man was tired, and another man in another room was now working on the verdict, for which they had both been waiting for the last two hours.

There was an air of calm; the plain-clothes man perused an old newspaper with outdated photographs of leaders who had been degraded in a single night; the last two days had created a certain intimacy between them; they were no longer strangers, and although one of them knew next to nothing about the other, neither would now be able to pass the other indifferently in the street.

They had been cooped up in this room together for two days; the plain-clothes man had ceased to be a real oppressor, and he had ceased to be a real victim; for the plain-clothes man he was an inconvenience, a thorn in the flesh, as their mutual contract had often been undermined over the past two days; the plain-clothes man now regretted he had failed to hold up his guard, had lowered it and come out of cover too soon, had lost his distance, let the distance be interrupted; he had lost some of his ascendancy, and lost it forever.

They sat face to face in silence, smoking cigarettes; as he kept fumbling for matches the plain-clothes man held out a lighter in his hand, and now he could not forgive himself for having been tricked into the gesture.

Yesterday had been different; when they took him hand-cuffed from home and down the elevator, it was totally different; they had absolute power over him. The cage quivered softly; when he slightly shifted his position, the drawing of a gallows leered up from behind his shoulders; the words Polish United Workers' Party were hanging from the noose; they spotted the drawing, exchanged looks; ha ha, one of them said, that's witty, that is, and instinctively he loosened his collar; they exchanged looks but they were too embar-rassed to erase it, and that was their first mistake the plain-clothes man now realized.

The cage walls quivered; the elevator stopped at one of the floors, an elderly man opened the door. Keep out, it's the militia, one of them barked, the man stopped dead in his tracks, as at a distant memory slowly raising his hands; the cage resumed its journey.

Then they sat in this room; that was their first day; the plain-clothes man put some questions, colleagues of his kept dashing into his room, how's it going, has he or hasn't he begun to give evidence, is he talking or isn't he, they kept asking, and then they would dash out again. He somehow doesn't want to talk, the plain-clothes man replied, it's rather tricky, he doesn't feel inclined.

— He doesn't feel inclined, eh? Then we'll see to it that he does — and they promptly rushed out, and there was not a shade of privacy between the two of them; with those brief appearances during the first hours they could operate officially and distantly.

— Any progress? Is he talking?

— He refused — the plain-clothes man replied; his moustache had a downwards droop which gave him an expression of immeasurable sadness; as they walked down long corridors to their present room he noticed that one in two of the young men here at headquarters sported the moustache that had been launched at the Gdansk shipyard eighteen months before.

— He's refusing to talk?

— Seems like it.

— Here's a piece of paper and a pen. Give a precise account of the last two weeks. Day by day. A precise account — he struck the sheet of paper against the table top, and then a sprinkling of ash glided down on a thread of light; he observed its descent and, for no reason, they both followed it with their eyes; silence fell for a moment.

— You have a good knowledge of French — the plain-clothes man said.

— No...pity... I don't. A few hazy notions. A bit of German. *Halt. Hende hoch...* From war films...

— You don't know French? Then how did you establish contact with the *service ronsainement* What? You know what it is? Do you mean to say you don't...

— What it is?

— You don't know? Let me refresh your memory. It's French espionage.

— There's no French espionage — he replied — That much I know for sure.

— No espionage, what do you mean? How can there be no espionage when there is? — the plain-clothes man slowly uttered, and fell silent.

— Here. On this paper you will give an exact account of your last two weeks. Day by day — the second man tapped his finger against the white paper.

— I refuse.

— So it's no?

— No it is.

The second man turned round and dashed out of the room; silence settled and lasted an instant; the door half opened again.

— You have three minutes. Stopwatch in hand. You have three minutes. Three minutes to make up your mind. Are you for the opposition or aren't you? Make up your mind — he flung his fist forward as though to strike, but wished merely to expose the watch on his wrist.

— You have three minutes.

He fixed his gaze intently on the window; the armoured car in the frozen courtyard down below had broken down and several soldiers were bustling helplessly around it; the lifeless town lay some distance beyond; a pile of snow was hardening on the pavement; a man stopped forlornly in the street, as if he could not find the way in his own town; in a bathroom a pensive woman was slowly washing her hair.

— One minute gone.

He said nothing; you have two minutes to go. Make up your mind. Are you with the opposition or aren't you? Again he was silent; a frozen drop twanged on the pane.

— What are you staring at that window for? What? What is there to stare at? — the other one asked.

— There are sparrows screwing on the windowsill. In winter...

Again the door slammed and they were left alone; you received dollars, we've got receipts in the cupboard, the plain-clothes man said, then fell silent.

— Dollars from French Intelligence?

— You know what I mean. Francs.

Now they were sitting face to face; the second day was beginning to slip away and the plain-clothes man felt that now he must speak.

— I went to Hungary. Last year...

—And?

— Prices have gone up. It's expensive.

Silence again settled between them; the plain-clothes man raised his head and stared at the ceiling; his pistol was rubbing nastily under his armpit.

— Salami, a hundred and ten forints. Ham, a hundred and ten. Cigarettes, fifteen. Mouth-organ, two hundred. Shoes, a few hundred.

— And matches?

— Matches? Don't know.

— You mentioned cigarettes.

— I have a lighter.

— What does wine cost?

— Ten forints.

—Tea?

— Packet or glass?

— Glass.

— Don't know. I took my own tea bags with me.

— What does a shirt cost?

— Two hundred and fifty.

— Did you go to the cinema?

—No.

— Really?

— Real... — he glanced at him in astonishment and fell silent; he was tired, and he longed for their ways to part.

He glanced at the plain-clothes man. — Not that long ago you were putting opponents of Gierek's regime behind bars.

— Well, yes. Of course.

— Where's the logic? You put them in prison then, you're still putting them in prison now. Then you lock Gierek up. And a couple of his cronies. Ultimately were those who opposed Gierek right or not?

— Well, sort of. Gierek's inside.

— Then how do you figure it all? Which side is guilty?

The plain-clothes man observed his desk at some length.

— You see. You see, we are basically fighting for the same cause... for the same cause... Only we fight from opposing camps. But we are fighting for the same cause... After all...

The door then opened, and the other officer stood on the threshold; he held an innocent white paper in his hand; the plain-clothes man gazed at him with hope and gratitude.

— So? — he exclaimed as he stood up; he stalked several paces from the desk, only then did he feel more at ease — So?

— We're taking him to Bialoleka. It's all signed.

— That's good. Off we go. Is there a car?

— Waiting downstairs.

— So everything's in order?

— Everything's OK.

— Good. Get your coat on — he tossed over his shoulder.

He stood up; he slung his jacket over his numbed shoulders and drew himself up to full height.

— Should we handcuff him? — the plain-clothes man asked; he spoke at a brisk pace now; he'd returned to routine.

— Whatever for? He can't escape. He's got nowhere to go.

— Well? — the plain-clothes man glanced at him. — Well?

He stretched out his hand and struck the switch with the flat of his palm; the bulb ceased to throb and hum; the corridor before him was full of light; he stood erect and slowly stepped into the glowing bright rectangle, into the chasm of a well, into a storm of locusts.

Freeze Frame Twelve

The pavement in the square in front of the Royal Castle stinks sourly of fresh tear gas, from the narrow side street rumbles a herd of wheelchairs; rickety ones, pushed by soldiers, chairs bounce and rattle; each soldier has at breast level two bewildered eyes, shining like medals.

The expedition, full of pitfalls, reaches its goal: the bus waiting at the curb, behind it a military van; in the eyes of the cripples relief flickers; the soldiers quicken their pace, driving away the pigeons stupefied by gas.

They surround the bus, grab the invalids in their arms; cap-peaks covering their shame, they crowd in front of the bus door.

A paralysed girl, for the last time in a man's embrace, senses a woman staring in consternation: — Good day, says the woman, what are you doing here, are you on a show tour? Some kind of excursion?

— I don't know anything — mumbles the soldier — I don't know anything, it had to be the square, so the square it is — his shaky legs climbing the steps, the smoked window hides the girl's blushes.

Two soldiers in battle dress furiously throw the wheelchairs onto the van; the cripples anxiously clutch the backrests of the seats; from the side street runs a soldier, out of breath; the wheelchair flies along the pavement; wait, men, please wait for us, wait; his passenger tries to cling to the speeding wheels with numb fingers, stop, wait, the engines gun, the woman turns and slowly goes away...

Czarnołęka: Black Meadow*

Shadow and silence cling to the cell; occasionally a rat prowls beneath the boards, but soon takes cover; from time to time the plumbing resounds with Eastern harmonics.

He stands with his back to the door. Before him is an iron grating; the trapped glaze of frosted air glistens between the bars; through its translucence he sees the exercise-ground, surrounded by barracks.

He stands with his back to the door; he did not go out into the yard today; he didn't have to go out into the yard today; it is one of the few things he can decide for himself, and he did not go out for exercise with the others today. The same yesterday, the same tomorrow.

The iron bars project themselves on the silhouettes of people circling the yard; each bit of grating squares its own man; he stands with his back to the door, watching.

*Czarnołęka (Black Meadow), an allusion to Białołęka (White Meadow), prison where the author and many other political detainees were held after the December 1981 declaration of martial law.

There is a rustling sound behind the low steel door as the flap of the spy-hole is raised; but the glass has been smeared with margarine and there is no way to check what is going on inside the cell.

The key makes a hoarse, guttural sound, then the brittle voice of the bolt sounds and the door opens; the screw stands in the doorway; he had planned to do a quick search and now looks at him in halting surprise. He takes a few steps, the boards rock and sway on the rotten joists, the screw peers round the cell with his ferret's eyes.

— What's up?

— Nothing... Just making sure the place isn't falling apart...

He walks up to the window, taps an enormous key against the windowsill, then picks up the bag abandoned on the bunk and greedily looks inside.

— What's up?

— Nothing... Just making sure the windows aren't falling apart.

He departs in a foul temper; the heavy door crashes against the frame, the steel air vibrates; he stands with his back to the door and hears the screw opening up the next cell.

He watches the prison yard through the grating; people circle round in cotton wool silence, prisoners from his cell among them. Prisoners of war.

They circle; the guards stand at the side, holding them on the leash of their eyes; their steel-grey overcoats are the colour of air and their silhouettes fade and vanish; the flat yard is intersected by crooked poles from which hang a mesh of barbed-wire like nerves, and a stunted tree that will beget no leaves.

The detainees circle; criminal offenders are in the barracks opposite; packs of cigarettes fly over the net close to their windows; they hook them on pieces of board removed from the bunks — each board has a nail at the end — so the packs can be spiked and carefully hauled inside.

— When are you getting out? — they shout, and the bars do not muffle the voices. — When are you going to put an end to all this nonsense?

A guard dashes out from behind the barracks; the windows of the criminal block slam shut; the screw snatches up the cigarettes and looks scathingly at the prisoners in the yard.

— Let 'em have those fags, they're Christians too. They're better Poles and Catholics than you.

—They're better Poles than you, the guard stutters.

A convict is pushing a wheelbarrow along the wire fence, a sweater comes flying towards him out of the window like a big shaggy bird and settles on the barbed wire; the convict delicately removes it with the haft of his spade and hides it among the concrete blocks in the barrow; he moves on, but promptly stops; the screw's clammy fingers fumble among the blocks and winkle out the garment; the prisoner stares, thinking of the punishment in store, or else with no thought at all.

He stands with his back to the door; he looks at the others dwarfed by the exercise yard and recognizes them at that distance without difficulty. He knows them.

The one who has stood still for a moment, looking towards the watchtower, is a famous old partisan; after World War Two, he specialized in breaking up Stalinist jails. He freed many people. But he will never succeed in smashing the prison where he is now ensnared. He was given seven death sentences — three were waived by amnesty. But he is still alive; he continues his walk, he is circling the yard.

That mousy one with thick specs and a hearing aid went deaf in Siberia where his mother gave birth to him. After concentration camp she was sentenced to lifelong deportation and didn't even teach her son Polish; they said he'd never have any use for it. When they came back he was several years old. In Moscow they had stood in a long gloomy line; she wanted him to have a look at that waxworks face. He returned, now he is circling the yard.

The stooping figure over there was once behind the barbed wire of a Nazi camp. He did not escape to freedom through the chimney; he returned by another route, he is circling the yard.

The man with the limp got a couple of years under Gomulka for a poem about the stupidity of Poles. At the trial they refused to believe that the poem was really by Jan Kochanowski [Renaissance poet]. He served his time for Kochanowski, was freed, now he is circling the yard.

That fellow over there was in the Warsaw Uprising at the age of fourteen, and when Poland was liberated, he was promptly given several years in prison. The indictment they read out stated that he had attempted to overthrow the new system of social justice. The lad chatting with him is still a schoolboy; he held different views from his teachers. Both are circling the yard.

The fellow in the sailor's jacket is a poet, he circles the yard thrashing out the rhythm of a poem.

Those two workers are recalling a trade union that no longer exists. It was swept away by war, yet the newspapers said all workers wanted another union that would be the only genuine one and would meet their demands. The workers circle the yard. That one is a printer who published the uncensored Milosz. For his work he received the writers' award. He could not collect it because he was in prison on a theft charge. He came out, but now he too is circling the yard.

That gesturing man refused to agree in 1968 that Mickiewicz should not be staged because he was antisocialist.* If he had disagreed with nothing else, he might have got away with a police thrashing. But he got several years. He came out. Now he is circling the yard.

*Adam Mickiewicz, Polish poet, dramatist, and political activist of the early nineteenth century. He is regarded as the national poet of Poland.

He turns away from the window, slowly takes one step, two steps. Then another few steps between the tiered bunks. Four steps in one direction, two to the side, four back, two to the side.

He is a writer, now he is circling round the cell; together with the others he is circling, circling...

Freeze Frame Thirteen

This conversation is being monitored... this conversation is being monitored... this conversation is being monitored... this conversation is being monitored... I am dreadfully tired, because I have been reading over a thousand pages of entries to a competition about the fate of couples a few years after their wedding and I feel completely shattered; there were several hundred entries mostly written by women, but it sounded as though they were written by a single woman, written by a single desperate woman, written by a single woman gone crazy from despair or a pathological liar; un-believable — all those marriages minted the same way, all those young people who talked themselves into the belief that they are basically entitled to be happy, and already the first few months, not even years, those wanderings through strange hovels costing the earth, living in the family flat with mother-in-law (who is always a plague), living apart and the meetings behind bushes, with a chance for a flat in the year two thousand, before retirement, children, who come into the world as if anybody needed them, a moment later and the husband starts to crack and is more and more often returning drunk; the warrior who cannot win any-thing, apart from those few printed ration cards for offal, for which his woman will get her ribs broken in the queue for shoes, which are unobtainable, for soap, which is enough for a couple of days, a few ration cards for life, which one cannot buy, because there is only getting up at dawn, drudgery, queues and the television news and maybe also queuing in front of the shop overnight, a shop where once upon a time they were selling fridges, or washing machines, and later, inevitably the first time you feel the fist of your drunken husband in your face; those women would eat the carpet for a wee bit of love, but usually they do not know the word; this exotic word, which nobody will ever explain to them, because this word has been obliterated from our language, killed in cold blood, this word *lov* ... this conversation is being monitored ... this conversation is being monitored ... this conversation is being monitored ... this conversation is being monitored ...

Breathless

The view from the window is moist and delicate, like an infinite distance in mist. But it is only a sheet stretched over the bars; it has to be doused with water, then it cools for a moment, only to be coated again in the mossy stifling steam that clings to the naked men sitting silent and breathless at the table.

The sun parches the barracks; every few minutes one of the men reaches for an aluminum mug, plunges it in the bucket, draws water and splashes it over his left shoulder on to the sheet with the gesture of someone breaking a spell.

He replaces the dented mug and returns to his thoughts without so much as a glance around, stretching.

The mug stands on the windowsill, its pale whiteness blurred against the shroud over the grating; the mug is covered all over in designs and tattoos; it has been retrieved from numerous mouths, and the date stamp tells that it has been thirty-one years in service. The sides are lined with lettering, naked women, dates, article and paragraph numbers that have broken the successive owners; someone reaches out again, draws from the bucket, splashes; the water spills onto the windowsill with a metallic clang, and the man puts the cup of bitterness aside once more as though it were an ordinary object.

The naked bodies at the table are overcome by languor and sweat; they sit in silence and slowly, intently breathe an air so empty that it no longer soothes the lungs.

Two hours more to midday — that is the hour of releases; it is at this precise hour each day that luck could strike; steps will be heard in the corridor that may well stop outside this door; with a whine of bolts the screw will appear in the doorway and grudgingly call out a name and turn his back before adding — get packed.

The one whose name is called will feel his pulse suddenly quicken; how shall I pack, where to, he reassures himself out loud; perhaps I'm being transferred, maybe they've brought charges, fuck 'em; probably a transfer. Or to give evidence at a trial.

— Now is the time for discharges. They take the convoy at eight a.m. — someone at the side says — but remember, once they came on the dot of ten...

The one whose name is called will excuse himself in this manner, he will suddenly let loose a great flow of talk, feverishly gesturing towards some objects that have to be packed, towards people whose names were not called; they will have to help him, as his fingers are too numb to hold on to anything for long.

It is the hour for discharges, but no one discusses the matter out loud; the scorching heat leaves them no strength for words; words today would be too heavy to utter.

Specks of dust melt into their bodies like snow, and they are silent; those who sit with their backs to the door keep a sharp eye on those who have the door in view; they can hear better. The cell door suddenly opens without a sound as though the hot metal had gone soft and the key could turn voicelessly in the lock; the guard has his cap tilted over the back of his head, rivulets of sweat stream from under the visor and down his face; he impatiently diverts them with the back of his palm.

He stands in the doorway looking at the seated men, then softly utters a surname.

The one whose name has been called rises slightly, then sits down; the screw knows that it is the hour for going free, so he persists in his silence, as though he fears the words might scald his lips.

— Well? Here I am...

The screw rubs his eyelids with the tip of his finger, from which the prison key is hanging like a huge wedding ring; he presses his eyelids carefully to verify that his eyes are still there, and speaks softly into his palms.

— For cross-examination.

The one whose name has been called now takes gentle breaths, he reaches for the aluminum mug, draws from the bucket.

— I'm not going for cross-examination.

—No?

—No.

He splashes water over the back of his shoulder and quickly sets aside the mug, which the water has not had time to cool.

— Who'd beat his meat in this heat? I'm not going. The screw stays put; he should have moved on, slamming the burning-hot door, but he stands on the threshold, and a pale man appears from behind his shoulders; his face as white as if the blood had drained out of him; won't you talk to me either? Eh? Don't you want to talk to me?

The one whose name has been called rises slowly, mechanically, without so much as a thought; he stands up, takes a few steps; but only as far as the door; he reaches for his shirt, which was wilting on the bunk, and he turns uncertainly around.

— My father — he says with an effort to the men seated at the table.

The door today is like rubber and emits no sound.

— Then I'll water the cloth. Until he returns.

— He said his father worked for the secret police. It was his first visit. They're not in contact. He didn't come on any of the visitors' days.

— So he gets a special visit. Took him unawares. That's why he went. They're not in contact. He went in a state of total confusion.

— He thought he was going to freedom. It's the time of day.

The thick felt of heat smothers their words, time ebbs and flows in all directions.

The cigarette smoke soaks up the last streams of air. The hour of freedom has not yet elapsed, and they feel its every tremor.

— Might as well tap next door. May someone's going out today.

— We'd hear if they did.

They are silent; the smouldering fag-ends corrode the metal of the tin, they sense the soft footsteps that cannot be heard from the corridor, the door moves in the salt-dry dust of the air, and the one whose name was called is standing in the doorway.

He throws his shirt back on the bunk; the sleeve slides slowly floorwards; he takes several steps; but only so far as the table; he picks up the mug, draws water from the bucket, splashes some onto the rag and drenches his hair with the rest, then seats himself on a stool.

— It was my father, he says at some speed, I told you my father works for the secret police. I have no contact at all with him. He did not come visiting because he knew I wouldn't want to speak to him. He took me unawares. That's why I went. I have no contact with him at all. I went in a state of total confusion...

— But it was a brief encounter...

The one whose name was called pulls a shrivelled cigarette from the pack and runs his tongue along the paper hull, leaving no trace of moisture. He rolls the cigarette in his finger; tobacco spills from under his nails.

— It wasn't an extra visit. It was a routine interrogation. There was another screw sitting there and they both wanted to cross-examine me.

He lights the cigarette, and its empty casing sparks with yellowish glimmers.

— My father screamed at me that I'm a fool to be inside here in this scorcher and that he can fix my release any time just so long as I sign the pledge of loyalty, and the other geezer said they need men like me to work with them, not sit in the jug.

— I said I refused to speak to them because they have blood on their hands. The other fellow blew his top and stormed out. I walked out too. My father yelled after me that I'm a fool and to stop being a fool, that he'd give me a colour TV as a peace offering. He never came visiting. He took me unawares. That's why I went. I have no contact with him at all. I went in a state of total confusion. I told them I refused to talk to them because they have blood on their hands. The other fellow blew his top and stormed out. I told you my father works for the secret police. He yelled after me that I'm a fool and to stop being a fool, that he'd give me a colour TV as a peace offering...

— Light up — one of them said and handed him a smouldering fag. — Light up. And then you can tell us everything...

— I have no contact...

— Light your fag. And douse the sheet.

The one whose name had been called reaches for the mug, but his hand is off the mark, and he has to turn round to measure his aim. Then he draws water from the bucket and splashes it over his shoulder; the piece of sheet is stiff as tin; the drops trickle down like mercury and patter against the windowsill.

The hour of discharges is coming irrevocably to a close; calm and resignation slowly spread among them, and the sensory threads that link them with the corridor begin one after the other to break.

And then the corridor suddenly returns to life; it fills with voices, bolts clap, footsteps approach.

— What's up? What's the row?

One of them stoops close to the door, avidly catches at the alarming, all but undecipherable sounds.

— Perhaps someone's being discharged? I wonder.

Tap next door.

The wall gives no reply; don't rap now, someone says, the screw's in there, wait a bit.

— They seem to be coming here — says the fellow by the door and takes a step back, the metal plate quivers on the door and stills; a man stands in the metal-framed threshold, with his shoulders all but propped against the plate, for the door has slammed behind him in an instant.

He stands dead-still and distrustfully inhales the unfamiliar air; in his hands he holds a bundle wrapped in a grey blanket, on which he precariously balances an aluminum bowl containing an aluminum plate and an engraved, dented aluminum mug; the sides are lined with lettering, naked women, dates, article and paragraph numbers of the laws that have broken the successive owners — Where're you from? he asks from the doorway.

— Here and there — the men at the table reply. — How about yourself?

— I'm a lecturer. They've brought in a whole convoy of us.

— Of university types?

— No. A mixed bunch, they've just brought us, the place is chock-a-block. Have you been inside long? — he looks around uncertainly.

— Pleased to meet you, prof. That bunk's free. Put your baggage down and take a peg.

— What baggage?

— That thing you're holding in your hands. Your bundle. Sit down, relax. Then you can tell us about yourself.

— Warm, isn't it? — the prof says slowly.

— Is that all you've got? Apart from state property?

— For months I'd kept a bag ready with all my stuff. To-day was the first time I didn't take it with me. And they picked me up from the college. Have you been in here long?

— Not that long, coming up to six months.

The prof sits on the bunk; the objects in the aluminum bowl rattle.

— How much longer will you be...

He rests his elbows on his knees, and his head inclines readily towards his palms.

They wait for him patiently, in silence.

— Things had got so much better of late; everything was sorting itself out, with the wife we were making a bit on the side, we were beginning to make ends meet; my wife works in the same institute where I'm a lecturer; a friend chucked it all in and started an artistic metalwork studio, he put us in the way of a tidy penny, gave us metal flowers to paint; after putting the children to bed my wife did the heads, and I added a splash of green; after a couple of nights' practice it went like a bomb, like a bomb... we began to recoup a little financially...we even started planning a holiday... I'd kept that bag ready for months...bitch of a world...

The hour of discharges is passed beyond recall; the one whose name had been called now reaches for the mug and knocks it impatiently on the bottom of the bucket.

— I'd kept that bag ready for months...it was going like a bomb...like a bomb...

Freeze Frame
Fourteen

The taxi driver passes his home; standing at the front door is his wife; he stops the cab and opens for her; the woman sits in silence; in old age you've become so boring, it makes me puke; he looks at her with vindictive satisfaction; I'll go to the hairdresser and have my hair dyed Chestnut No. 5, shouts the desperate woman, sure that she'll change her life; have your ass dyed Chestnut No. 5, he answers soothingly; you bastard, have you seen a broad with a prick; what broad, what are you talking about; if you can't see, then you'd better look at your wedding picture; she slams the door, and he pulls away; both of them will have a fine day.

Why does the old man spit in the face of the young one who jostled him?

Why does the pregnant woman, who tried to jump the queue at the butcher's to get a piece of meat, stumble out of the shop, tears rolling down on to her prominent stomach, and the words coming after her to trip her swollen legs: shouldn't have screwed around, wouldn't have a belly-full now, you...

Why does the doctor twist the old woman's arm and back while shoving her out of his office?

The hatred cultivated in the people of this country does not allow them to think; the unrelenting hunt for victims leaves no time for it, and the government really no longer needs to reform the nation...

Prison Sickness

The night's silence runs cold in the cell. Motionless shadows wilt on the walls.

The window grating is overgrown with a thick mesh that guards the inside and suppresses sounds. The loathsome Alsatian can't be heard — it thrashes about between the fence of thorn and the sky-high wall, which is daubed over with flaking white paint to the height of a prisoner's upraised arms, exposing previous layers from the Gomulka and Gierek eras; it is a young prison.

Bitter stars spilling out of the narrow tape of sky cannot squeeze through the steel mesh.

A scant rustling sound can be heard the other side of the low metal doors. The screw eavesdrops for a while, then delicately raises the tin shutter of the spy hole and peers in. There in the even darkness bunks are stacked high. The grey fold of a blanket slides to the floor. Someone's palm shows white. The warped aluminum mug absorbs the faint gleam from the other side of the window.

The luminous spot on the sheet-metal door fades out. The screw has done his duty; he certainly won't be overlooked for promotion.

He lies motionless, supporting his head on his numbed hand; he really should change position. Instead he moves his head only slightly, taking in the cell with his gaze; and now he sees the grating with its metal veil and the high prickly hedge beyond, the other side of which is a strip of meticulously raked desert sand and the hound and that wall, daubed over in white paint to the height of a prisoner's upraised arms. The wall is searched by a probing light; under the glare white paint flakes off without a sound...

He lies motionless. The stillness is disrupted by voices floating over from the barracks, which is invisible through the grating. They soak through the grating and reverberate from the walls, pillars and bends. The other block is at communal prayer. The prisoners open all the windows and garbled words mix confusedly in the night, amid which snatches of songs, hymns and choruses float out like bubbles and burst. Again the prisoners can't agree on a single version: Father — Lord God, Thou'rt Poland — Poland's not perished yet — we'll not desert — as long as Poles — God rest their souls — the priest chased Katie — the crow won't the eagle — whence our nation came — we shall regain — dragged out by night —...After a moment the bazaar of voices drifts away like a frigate on the wind, and now only single words flutter in the mesh; the hound slinks off with its tail tucked under.

He lies motionless. His head slides off his hand and he instantly feels sharp little needles of blood darting into his fingers, which slowly return to life. He begins to move his fingers. He moves his hand between the folds of the blanket and chances on some scraps of paper and envelopes and book covers. The cover that he now touches is cool and thick: the blue binding of a notebook from which the inside was ripped out a few hours back during the search. The covers are now without the written pages, but some vestiges and fragments of jotted sentences and words still swirl in their midst, cling to them: two worlds — a shop trainee showers people standing in line with orangeade and hides, laughing, behind the empty shelves; no one reacts; many newspapers carry reports on the bear that has shown up in the Tatra, it is affectionately referred to as *teddy*, and a special correspondent reports on it for the *Express*; on Polish radio there's a program '*teatime round the Samovar*', Polevoy, editor-in-chief of *Yunost*, is dreaming of a trip to Eastern Siberia, he tells the legend of how Siberia was created by God, who felt tired one day and tipped out a whole bagful of wealth, he also tells how the Germans wanted to blow up the monastery on Jasna Gora and put the blame on the Russians, the Russians however found out about this diabolical plan and thank God, as Polevoy puts it, saved the monastery; a man in the shop stuffed a frozen goose under his shirt, you won't squeal, he asks his neighbour in the line; mister, they must come, sure as two and two is four, they'll come for sure, ask anyone you like, they want to anyway, they fucking well do, they'll leave only stones behind, they must come in the end, those Chinks; we average women ought always to be cheerful; assent to falsehood is the root of evil in the country — from the testament of Ryszard Siwiec of Przemysl: lawyer and soldier in the Home Army, who set fire to himself in the stadium during Gomulka' s speech at the harvest festival; he was protesting against the invasion of Czechoslovakia; one thousand eight hundred tons of powdered milk from West Germany forwarded to prisons and old people's homes on the contention that they contain dangerous hormones; the institute that issued the pronouncement turned out not to have the equipment for such tests; Norwid — where energy outdistances intelligence, there's a massacre every generation; a criminal prisoner, a robber turned trusty, sixth year inside, says a good thing we've got martial law, there'll be some order at last, lately a fellow was afraid even to go out onto the street; Marek, already nodding off on his bunk, in a state of half-sleep, once I'm in Canada the first thing I'll do is go to a shop, you can get everything in the shops there, and I'll buy myself a kilo of communism and every evening I'll give it a fucking great battering with a hammer, till the day I die; those empty notebook covers; scraps of jotted sentences slowly fade, the covers grow cold and harden, and a vigilant plain-clothes policeman is now bent over a wad of torn-out pages.

He lies motionless, the numb hand slowly regains feeling, painfully, as after a bout of prison sickness, but the head does not move; half-dropped eyelids; he can just see the man behind the bars; the blind light from above the wall presses through the window and projects a shadow of the lad who climbs gingerly down from the upper bunk so as not to wake the cripple sleeping beneath; he's reached the floor now, for the bunks, arranged on rotten planks, begin to shake; he raises the lid of the bucket, draws some coffee and drinks avidly; the warm stimulant diffuses lazily through his veins; the man pauses and stands stock-still, straining his ears; out in the corridor he hears a key rattling in the lock of the grating which separates this corridor from the duty-room; the grating drops and the screw won't be able to open it again until morning, as the key is taken from him for the night; he won't appear in the corridor again this shift. A stormy day ends on the consumptive rattle of iron bars; when hours ago two inmates were led out on their successive journeys into the unknown, several hundred men began to bang their aluminum dishes against the bars; that orgy of sounds, unending, in a vacuum disrupted by the prison siren wailing its alarm call; those who're in cells at the wall end and don't know what's going on in the yard, listen greedily; the din of vibrating dishes dies violently down, the cell door opens suddenly and a gang of police crashes in; their helmeted heads make them look like motorcyclists on their way to a country brawl; the short-legged captain punctuates his words with his white baton; we've put up with so much so long, it's all up now, we'll give you a fucking what for, see, a right fucking what for, see, all out now, hurry; greedy hands in the corridor fumble bodies and tear at clothes, a hob-nailed foot is raised as if to give a kick in the belly, but the energetic boot merely strips the trousers off instead; the man now stands naked; a camera is heard to hiccough; one of the motorcyclists has put his baton aside and takes photos, others charge into the cell and hide behind the doors.

Afterwards the cell is alien and inaccessible. They slowly enter, pause; blankets, clothes, papers and books are stacked on the bunks, the scrap of cable and two razor blades that could be connected to the light flex for boiling water have vanished; the cupboard has spilled out its guts and helplessly spreads its wings, an onion rolls about on the floor. The place now seems strange, one must first re-acclimatize before one can restore remembered shapes, as one does after a forced move.

He had then sat on the bunk, leaned his head on his hand, and when night came, no one in the cell let him know.

The other man burrows into his bunk and falls silent; a transparent vein of light collects flickering beads of dust; his hand, now restored, wanders through the dunes of the blanket; his fingers encounter rustling pages, stray among words so familiar that they can be read from the relief of the letters; what can I write you, how can I write you, I'm seldom in Warsaw, this town is hell; so are others, only different; I feel that without our meetings in Przechodnia Street an important point has ceased to exist in my mental geography; would you like any books, how about some English ones; learn a language, because otherwise you'll go mad; well then, Lopucha has sat down to write you a letter twice already, she sat down, gripped her pen, the paper's on the table, and then what, nothing came of it; wondering what could, what would, and nothing comes into her head; and now I drink to your health, your good spirits and Wyspianski's 'Liberation'; it's so difficult to write to you, because I don't know how one writes to people who've come a cropper, who can't break loose from their own thoughts; then there's always the question whether what we are doing has any sense; by the way, I should mention that the Metropolitan Commander of the Citizens' Militia has no influence on the functioning of the postal services, nor therefore on the times at which mail is delivered; he sits up on the bunk for the first time in hours; first sweeps up everything around him, then fishes out from the pile books, shirts, letters, socks, a matchbox, photographs, bird feathers, a sweater; with precise movements he sets all his belongings in the old places he had so far been unable to retrieve in his memory. Then he smoothes out the blanket, chances on a cigarette in its folds, lights it, quietly descends from the bunk and calmly pees into the bucket.

He sits down by the table to smoke and shakes the ash over his left shoulder outside the bars.

He is smoking, then reaches to where the empty tin always used to stand and where the lump of margarine always lay; he fills the tin with margarine, reaches round his neck and rips the strap off his prison shirt, pushes it into the margarine; a match flickers. The tin comes suddenly to life, as though a swarm of luminous white ants had come seething out of it; he reaches under the bunk to the place where the cardboard box always used to be and screens the pulsing source of life from those who are sleeping.

He sits at the table; on the box is an exotic label: the name of some Paris factory, shop or institution with the address and telephone number. Avenue Franco-Russe — he recalls that street from a previous life; the Franco-Russian street, it intersects Avenue Rapp; that is where the gas-line is supposed to end; one day the red Siberian gas will gush out and suffocate all the pathetic fools who have done nothing to deserve their city.

He reaches for the binding where the notebook always used to be; he opens it, silently. Those scraps of sentences and words, now irretrievably locked within his card-index, appear and return, jostling their way back, they're there.

Just another stretch of the arm to where the piece of paper always lay and where it lies again; it's covered on one side in print — a list of things from the Austrian parcels that were distributed here by the Polish Red Cross; the Austrian National Committee for Aid to Polish Detainees, gifts of the Austrian Red Cross. A sanitary package for women. One soap, 1 toothpaste, 1 washing powder, 1 shampoo, 1 package for female hygiene, 250 grams of cotton wool.

He turns the sheet over, it glints with dazzling whiteness; then he takes a ballpoint from his pocket and stoops over the wick to prevent the glow shimmering on the pane and arousing the guard who watches behind his back in the high tower above the wall.

He leans forward.

The night's silence runs cold in the cell. Motionless shadows wilt on the walls.

The loathsome Alsatian can't be heard — it thrashes about between the fence of thorn and the sky-high wall, which is daubed over with flaking white paint to the height of a prisoner's upraised arms, exposing previous layers from the Gomulka and Gierek eras. This is a young prison.

Bitter stars...

Freeze Frame Fifteen

...The alien railway station, ceiling vanishing somewhere into the heights, feet cold on the stone floor; no hopeful goodbyes or greetings bring relief.

Sly cameras shamelessly stare into faces, deaf tunnels greedily swallow people up, the air has a regular beat.

The jealous information windows are mum; an unobtrusive queue hugs the wall by the newspaper stand with its loud titles: *Merry-Go-Round, Land of Soviets, My Home, World of the Deaf, Poland, Party Life, Nutrition, Let's Live Longer, Soviet Woman, Poland with Wings, Livestock Breeding, From the Battle Front, Literaturnaya Gazeta, For and Against, Poland in Russian, Here and Now, Problems of Peace and Socialism (Russian edition), The Woodland Voice, Do-It-Yourself, Soviet Lights, Mental Health, Public Health, Generation, Pig Breeding, Together, At Friends, Defense Knowledge, Izvestia, Discover the World, For Freedom and People, Intensive Therapy, Young Communist Pravda.* The soldiers' weapons shine, and their hobnailed boots echo.

A roar rises to fill the ceiling; carriages spill out gangs of reservists with eyes white from vodka; they throng the platforms, clinging to each other, stunned by the illusion of freedom, bloodied in numerous skirmishes; gaudy banners whisk about, giving dates, platoon numbers and localities; a nervous patrol, which stretches an invisible string along the platforms, turns a blind eye. Yells of demobbed at last, more than one cunt shed a tear, the howls echo; the reservists, who have already fulfilled their commendable December duties, mix with the conscripts, stupefied by drink; their vacant eyes search for the right trains to take them towards their new functions and duties. *Mama, come to my induction,/Sergeant-Major sends his card;/Bum grenade blew my hand off,/Come and see, this is your blood.* Bellowing of drunken throats; a train draws out, a conscript hanging out of a window, and the vomit streams along the car like an azure veil; a drunken girl flings herself after the carriage, whimpering. She runs, her bluish calves flicker; crashing into a pylon, she slides down, leaving on the concrete a trail of blood, phlegm and tears...

1985 and after...

Empty...Sort of

The taxi driver went up to the duty-room on cotton wool legs and stood quietly before the blurred pane with the round aperture. He twirled his cap in his hands and looked coaxingly at the duty-officer, who sat with his head collapsed on his chest. He looked like a man overcome by insurmountable drowsiness. But he was simply stooped over a small mirror set on his knee. A scrap of newspaper with a rosette of coagulated blood stuck to his upper lip; he was delicately trying to prize it away with the nail of his little finger.

— Excuse me, Sir, if you please... — said the taxi driver, as he bowed low and froze in timeless obeisance.

The duty-officer shuddered and violently raised his head. The congealed drop of blood remained on his nail, a soft clank resounded under the table, and simultaneously atoms of light flashed in the semidarkness.

— Seven years' bad luck — the taxi driver sheepishly volunteered, but was instantly scared by his own voice. The duty-officer looked at him, but manifested no irritation, as the scarlet streak that now joined the gash to the corner of his mouth caused him to smile rapaciously with half of his face.

— Well? — the duty-officer spoke. — Wha'?

— How to... — the taxi driver at one jerk whipped off his cap — How to...I mean...is there any other exit?

— Wha'?

— I've got a passenger here, tall, cap, overcoat, I mean... said he'd be gone two minutes, but my meter's already clocked up a thousand seven hundred...and it's chilly...so maybe there's another exit here, or how...

— No one of that description came in 'ere today — the duty-officer said, grinding the glass with his boot.

— What d'ya mean no one of that description, when I saw him go in with my own eyes — for a moment the taxi driver lost his head, then instantly simmered down — I saw him go in. Cap and overcoat. Eight a.m. What time's it now? A thousand seven hundred on the meter. Chilly...isn't there another exit here, or...

— No one of that description came in 'ere today. Wait 'ere quietly or else go home. What I says I says. Yes or no. Got it?

The bewildered taxi driver reeled towards the door: what d'ya mean, no one came in when I saw him go in, had an overcoat, said stay put and wait, what d'ya mean when I tell you I saw him go in...it's like a movie, dammit, like a movie...a cap...

Two people passed him who without looking round proceeded along the familiar route to the blurred pane with the aperture. The taxi driver eyed them suspiciously and retreated to the door; it'll soon make a thousand seven hundred and forty...seven hundred and forty. — Cold, eh?

The two men then tackled the stairs, the repellent metal netting climbed upwards above the banisters. The duty-officer sat behind the glass, staring down at the floor, at the carmine mouth of the actress whose photo had come unstuck from the broken mirror. One might have thought he was blowing on his cold fingers. But he was only holding the receiver in his huge palm and reporting in dulcet tones — It's the, it's them two literary blokes was sent for...

And now they were instinctively but unnecessarily raising their heads to read the nameplates fastened above the doors, as they made their unerring way to the correct one.

They stopped outside, and when one of them raised his hand to knock, the door slid away from his fingers. For a moment they stood eye to eye, saying nothing, then they heard the instruction: I'm too busy right now, kindly wait on that bench for a while, we can have a chat later; they turned away towards the bench, retreating under an escort of eyes. Then they sat down and simultaneously leaned back on the bench as though a gust of wind from the closed doors had pushed them there.

They were silent, and the hard keyboard of the typewriter could be heard rattling away from the other side of the door.

Then for a long time the glow-lamp hissed beneath the ceiling, regularly died down, then returned after a moment. One of them took a newspaper from his pocket and glanced at the door, the other twirled a cigarette in his fingers spilling bits of tobacco, then placed it in his mouth without lighting up. They sat in silence, hemmed in by words that had already erupted earlier that day, on their way to this place.

They had been standing in a tram car that dragged itself across the bridge so slowly the water beneath did not stir; it was in the paper, one of them said, about reducing the speed limit, people are inconvenienced by the noise, which in our language means the bridge is in danger of collapse; then the tram stopped and the door-wings flapped; smoke was belching from under the first wagon and when they got out, they saw a little woman in a tram conductor's cap rampaging down the car and yelling to the passengers, run for your lives, it'll be a right ballsup un' I don't know who's gunna pay, and as though to emphasize her words she banged the fire extinguisher on the asphalt; the extinguisher emitted a prolonged whistle, then after the last thump the bottom fell out, spilling a handful of rust from inside; people peered curiously under the car and for the first time that day their faces were creased with laughter; it's a sight for sore eyes, they whispered among themselves, smoking like the devil.

The two made for the river bank walking slowly, watching the exuberant water below; they passed the bays and the bridge ebbed away — I've never been so hamstrung by censorship as now, never; for the last couple of years it's been different, especially now; the old censor could be fooled in thousands of ways; the game could be fun, could be humiliating, but I don't know how to tackle this one; he's inside me, and he keeps getting stronger; he was pretty strong way back in '80 and '81, but in those days you simply waited, you could still suppress all your inner doubts; my censor made himself known in earnest when I was in jail; all those previously diffuse and elusive elements were concentrated in one place, several hundred people; it was a colony of apes; at first I resisted that image and rejected my own evaluation, but then the image took hold; besides, I wasn't alone. They hauled in a sober-minded bloke from the Poly and after a couple of days, he realized how nauseated I was by all that jingoism, all that ritual and religious singing every day through the bars, stirring up the entire prison to a hunger strike every other minute on the least pretext, and I saw great tub-thumpers who noshed at night on the quiet and broke those fasts of theirs after two days; that ranting on for months on end about high-level politics, and "the spring will be ours" even though the spring went on relentlessly; the division between those who held that the greatest service to the country was to take the mickey out of the screw and those who went to give the screws the season's greetings: that'll give 'em something to think about, they'd say, and so another month was twaddled away; plus those symbols, symbols of something that no longer existed, because people didn't have it inside them in the first place; so that sober bloke from the Poly started telling how a legend was growing up about our prison in the outside world, people were saying that the extreme of the extreme had been rounded up here; as a rank-and-file activist he was glad they'd taken him, he stood to learn a lot here in this academy of the opposition; that's what he called it, now he's just wondering how the whole business could ever have lasted sixteen months; he couldn't get over his amazement as he looked on and observed how a respectable union activist was happy if he caught sight of a secret policeman in the yard, because he could shout at him from a safe distance, you bastard, you broken prick on duck's legs; he watched and was amazed and wondered what could be gained by all that; he looked at those people who gobbled the chocolate from foreign parcels and then listened to children's stories about ration cards for two hundred grams of lemon drops, and that was an excuse for preaching about the ruthlessness of the authorities; he beheld a once-important guru whose mental laziness prevented his reassessing his view of his own importance; once he had conducted discussions about how the system encourages and fosters alcoholism, how the system depends on it, and here he had now discovered a way of distilling moonshine, and distilled it on the sly; he saw those who'd wanted to hang grafters now giving bribes to the man in charge of the baths who was serving a sentence for corruption, and for a douceur you can whistle a shirt with the prison stamp; it can be smuggled through at visiting hours; the women outside like to sport a grey shirt with the prison sign as a gesture of mourning; he saw them grumbling to the Swiss doctors from the Red Cross who've already seen a prison or two in Asia and South America; he heard them complaining that the water in the baths was too hot or too cold, he saw men who only recently had ordered others to paint graffiti about television lies, now sucking up to the screw so he'd let them watch the news out of turn; he saw politicals who treated the convicts with contempt; there were a couple of professional crooks in prison with us who went on hunger strike in sympathy, and it was entered in their personal files which would follow them through all the prisons of the land all their lives long, he saw people who were happy to be in prison and did not notice their halo was of scurf; so that sober-minded fellow told me that, though he considers himself to be a cultured type, he would formulate his view as follows — namely, he wouldn't give a shit for such an academy of opposition. Obviously not everything there was so bad, there were lots of different people, but somehow it all got blurred and that ghastly image prevailed; I ended up not writing a single word about those days, because either my censor would have made a liar of me unto death, since you simply couldn't write about such things; the idea was to build morale and boost myths regardless, and for a book like that — had I ever got round to writing, I'd have received the Ministry of Culture prize at least, or worse. Besides, what publisher would have printed it? I'd have been treated like a provocateur or police spy...

They paced their walk slowly from bay to bay, as the bridge receded, and they were soon to stand on firm, hard ground. — I find reading difficult, I pick up a book with a sense of nausea; it looks as though the garbage dump will become literature, and nothing else will remain, all those hundreds of pages, thousands of poems, memoirs, diaries, impressions, notes, all very soulful and high-minded, those sufferings endured with slimy satisfaction; how many more years is this to be our nourishment? Those December nights, wars declared on the entire nation, nothing less would do, tanks, handcuffs, armoured cars, troops going out on the street, all those stage props, even private dreams under martial law, and children's thoughts for posterity; that specific language one is duty-bound to use if one wants to belong; it's our own newspeak; those internment camps, reds, bolshies, underground broadsheets, police ambushes, raids; even those held in unbarred rooms in vacation centres refer to them as cells and camps; loss of freedom is not enough, what matters is the rig-out; when I read all that stuff I feel like puking, there's not so much as a thought on the horizon; like throwing petrol bombs at water-cannons, and there's no breaking free, for there's no tolerance here; pathos excludes tolerance and we're getting close to using hopeless propaganda, just one step from the method and gimmicks of the other side, just one step from their mentality and stereotypes, their stultification and absolutism; one mag had the guts to discuss these problems; people started shouting that it was a secret police job and I don't know if the publication's still coming out; it all makes me puke, I've had my own small part in it, but I'll probably pack it, though it's difficult to go it alone, to hell with all this foam-beating; up-fingers is the only universally adopted program to be invariably shown, that's our form of salute...

They stopped for a moment and rested against the rail.
— I'd gladly toss a coin into the water, one of them said, it might help me reassess a couple of problems, for either I calmly go on considering myself the aristocrat of literature, or else I finally admit that the literary backwater, that provincial homespun stuff, is me; that's really what our literature is; our whingeing behind prison bars and our ob-

tusely menacing squeaks about the spring being ours sound like poetry to us; we have nurtured censors within us who have outstripped us and our thoughts and write on our behalf about this country; we're happy from time to time to get a parcel from abroad with a kilo of sugar, a kilo of flour and some toothpaste; we'd gladly frame the parcel as documentary proof that Europe remembers and admires Polish literature; admirable people, noble nation gone to the dogs, we describe it in our own blood, but we write on blank cards dealt out by our censor; it was this censor who prevented my writing that I didn't want any hero's testimony; everyone in my prison was handed a testimony; a souvenir for life, they said with emotion, a pass to history, they said hysterically, good typographic design and half-bound what's more...

They reached the tram stop on the bridge that joined the two banks and suddenly stopped talking, as though they felt hard ground underfoot. One of them pointed at the colossal building and the huge red flag full-sail above it, and white-capped young men milling all around. And we'll carry on about how they sit there plotting which scenario to apply, but in the event we shall die standing, not on our knees. The wheels screeched. Their tram rolled up to the stop in a veil of smoke. Clearly the woman with the conductor's cap falling over her eyes had lost heart and was now staring indifferently ahead with blank expression. They boarded and the tram car immediately dissolved in a black fog.

Afterwards they sat in silence. One of them put his newspaper away, and the other drew out his next cigarette and crushed it between his fingers. It was the twentieth cigarette he had not lit during the long hours waiting on the bench that day.

The glow-lamp hissed beneath the ceiling, the light flared, then expired. A man in overalls appeared in the aisle. He walked swiftly towards them, and drew up suddenly in passing.

— Just a moment — he said without giving them a look.

They sprang up in surprise; two more steps, two more steps, one more, said the man, and when they had moved a little to the side he pushed the bench away. Behind it there was a small metal door in the wall, which he opened. He took a screw driver from his pocket and started fiddling among the cables, tapping the microphone head. Then he glanced at them and at the cables again and shrugged his shoulders.

— What the fuck do they want? he muttered, — Everything's OK.

He slammed the metal door, pushed the bench back in place and made off. He turned round for one moment longer and flung over his shoulder — Quiet, aren't we?

Then the door opened and there stood the man who'd ordered them to wait. — As it happens, he said I'm quite snowed under, so we might as well call it a day. Should the occasion arise, then of course...— He tapped his finger against the door-frame and closed the door behind him.

Exhausted and relieved, they went downstairs slowly.

— I began to feel the urge, — one of them said, — it's a neat situation to describe, but I thought you might want to.

They descended to the landing and turned into the broad staircase. — I did have the urge, only I thought less in terms of situation than of storyline, besides I thought I'd let you have it as you might feel inclined, — the second one said, and that we'd sort it out between us when we left...

And they both started laughing and laughing, and they came to the room where the duty-officer sat behind the blurred aperture, and still they were laughing; the pale taxi driver stood muttering to himself by the wall. — He must have come in, I saw him with my own eyes, I've clocked up four thousand two hundred, four and two hundred; you definitely didn't see him? he shouted to the duty-officer in despair. But the latter looked at the men laughing, pulled the visor over his eyes and lifted his head, because he could now see them only knee-high.

— What're ya laughin' at, huh? Who're ya laughin' at?

— Ourselves — one of them replied.

Quietly they closed the heavy door behind them.

— Well — the duty-officer shook his fist after them.

— Well. Loonies, eh? — he turned to the taxi driver.

— No, no, it's from Gogol — the taxi driver instinctively mumbled.

The National Theatre's Burning Down

A banner of flame streams from the National Theatre and is smothered in smoke. Sanguine pigeons sway above the marsh of rooftops like small black sails and search frantically for their old roosts.

At the roof's edge several firemen clutch a limp hose, waiting for water. They lift their legs above the abyss like cancan girls as the sheet iron burns their soles. The firemen glance indifferently at the eyes frozen in admiration below, eyes that gaze in horror: a fireman has mis-stepped and beats his arms as if to warm himself. But it's clear that he's flapping his arms to regain his balance, and his life. The crowd groans relief as, in the last instant, the fireman grabs the flabby hose, straightens up, spits into the fire, and glances down at the street.

The low sky is propped on billowing pillars of smoke. In the theatre square motionless red cars and yellow watering-vans with snowplows secured to their fronts deliver water from the town. Large-helmeted firemen storm among the cars and the swirl of hoses; a string of police separates them from the crowd. The policemen are young and eager, their visors screening the curiosity and desperation in their eyes; they're not allowed to face the raging fire, nor to take a single step forward. So they stand in a trance, questioning the people's faces, trying to discover what is going on behind their own backs. They do not see the small group of actors in fantastical costumes driven out of rehearsal by the flames, and who now give feverish interviews to the camera: — I was just standing there, and suddenly the stage rode up in the air, and there was a great swoosh, and I just fled. And now I'm not budging an inch from here.

— And I even lost my shoes, I've got no shoes, oh god, I've lost my shoes — another one keened, forever pointing at his feet. — See what I mean, I don't even have shoes. What a fizzle.

— As for myself, in all honesty, I thought the ventilation'd turned on again, so I shouted to them to turn it off, what a hope, some ventilation that is, heaven help us.

— Our home sweet home's on fire — the actors now cry, and gather like a small flock of exotic birds. That last shout pierces the ranks of the vigilant militiamen and reaches the crowd; people nod their heads in approval and look at each other knowingly. — That's it, that's it, fire's a vicious element, say what you like.

— A flaming red fire, begging your pardon.

— Hey, listen — a man in the crowd chips in — you know, at ten a.m. Radio Free Europe said it was burning, so I dashed along, and the fire started at half past twelve. So how could they have known at ten? Because extremists told them their plans beforehand, but couldn't keep on schedule. It's all clear. The underground did it. And how! How could they know...

People turn their gaze from the fire, lower their heads, adjust to the sudden dimness and look for the man who'd been speaking, but he surfaces elsewhere, emerges from the crowd, explains heatedly, gesticulating, pointing behind him.

— That lot heard Free Europe giving news of the fire at ten a.m. They can confirm it. And the fire broke out at half-past twelve, now didn't it? Everybody heard.

— Well, sort of — uncertain voices respond.

— So what the hell's going on here? — someone reflects out loud.

— Extremists set it alight. The underground. Simple, ain't it?

— Just which undergound are you talking about? It's obvious who did it. Mijal's gang. Anyone can tell you that.

— But Mijal's in the jug. It was in the papers.

— Right you are. When were you born? It's like talking to a small child. So what if he is? He's got a network all over Poland. Every national theatre will go up in flames now. First it was the castle, now the theatres, next the... He who steals an egg will steal an ox, you mark my words.

—And Kuroń, he said not to burn committees. To build committees — someone says, then becomes petrified and breaks into nervous uncontrollable laughter.

— It's the undergound what done it.

— What bullshit he talks. It's provoca...

— There's different ways of looking at it — people start putting two and two together.

— When the fire broke out, Bujak was seen in disguise. Sure was.

— Who saw him?

— Everyone...

— You did too?

— I didn't actually, I came late. Everyone else did though. He was in uniform to dodge the police. He's grown a beard. Just slipped past.

Suddenly a tapering flame cuts through the film of smoke. A group of women suddenly begin to wail like orphans: — *God that hast Po-o-o-land throughout all the ce-e-enturies* — the choir swells, the song drifts like smoke only to fall an instant later, the words become unhinged and disjointed, and quarrelsome voices can be heard again — it's not allowed, the primate forbade us to sing *Give us back our free land,* so what if he did? seeing it's not free anyway, let's sing as it comes, we're not to sing, sing bless oh Lord, the primate said not to sing that version, but the correct one — smoke stifles the fretful voices, people watch as the last victims descend the tapering ladder. Trapped by the fire, they'd been patiently waiting at the windows to be rescued; at the foot of the ladder the commander admonishes a smoke-black fireman guarding the only escape route — For chrissake, don't let 'em in, let 'em out, don't let 'em in — The fireman stands to attention, senses the numerous eyes focused on him and blinks uncertainly at the crowd. — Firemen aren't up to much nowadays, they used to be better-looking, more like men, they're not up to much nowadays, flashy uniforms all right, they were better-looking before...

— They used to get plenty of sauerkraut and pease pudding in the old days. More lime, better teeth. Now there's less lime. And no sauerkraut to be had for love or money.

Drunk at this early hour, a man hoists a baby in a polyester jump suit aloft to show him the fire, — Let the kid learn from the cradle — he explains to his neighbours; the frisky infant in his slippery outfit keeps sliding out of the man's uncertain grip — For all the world like a little eel, a slippery little eel — the man says admiringly.

Exhilarated by the crowd, two young girls at his side quite unashamedly read a crumpled clandestine newssheet; the miniature rheostats rise and fall with their breasts.* — Here, says one with flushing cheeks, — Here, Solidariusz has won, see? Solidariusz has won! It all began in '83, when Mr Jagiello decided to give his son the names Przemyslaw Solidariusz. The People's Council refused to register him, invoking the opinion of the Linguistic Culture Committee. Then there was a schism. Chairman Professor Szymczak objected to the name Solidariusz, while the vice-chairman and two members of the Presidium backed the child's father. The case went to the Chief Administrative Court. Mr Jagiello won, but the People's Council still refused to register the name.

*Electrical circuit controllers worn to signify resistance to the regime after Solidarity badges were banned.

The father appealed and despite fierce resistance on the part of the prosecutor, the court again recognised the father's claim. The People's Council finally gave way and the boy was officially named Solidariusz.

— The ranks of our defense grow day by day — people mutter admiringly. There's nothing they're afraid of. Now they'll seize the stick. The proverbial stick. We've already done our share of the fighting.

— Old folks won't be laying down arms that easily. Oh, no, they won't. We'll show 'em the stuff we're made of. Tit for tat, a stick for a stick. Why, it can't be more than an hour ago, women began making a cross of flowers, under the eyes of the police, but they only had enough flowers for one arm. With the police watching 'em. If we had more flowers, we'd give 'em what for...

— Some fire that.

— First they start a fire, now they'll pretend there's no water to extinguish it. They've brought the plows out. The snow plows, I ask you.

— There's more than one way of looking at it. At any rate the director's office knew nothing, because the managing director was cut in half by the safety curtain, in the presence of witnesses; there's an iron curtain like I'm saying in case of fire, or rather there was, because it's melted now; the director dashed forward to lower it and seal off the flames, but the ropes burned through and whang bang it chopped him in two on the spot, in two equal halves it did; one half was consigned to flames, the other to water, courtesy of the fire brigade. It's tragic, I must say.

— It's an act of God. 'Cause a couple of years ago that director said on the radio that Witkacy committed suicide on hearing that the Germans had invaded Poland.** That's divine judgement for you. He had another two years to go, not a bad run for his money if you ask me. He just made the centenary and then croaked.

— The angel wingsin the costume wardrobe are burned to a frazzle.

— Hussars' wings, not angel wings.

— There's no Hussar wings, what rubbish you do talk. Angel wings, I tell you. Quite apart from the fact that lots of people have been burned. Couldn't escape in time, burned to a frazzle. And people of standing what's more.

— See the women with a portrait of St Florian, the fire doesn't seem so bad over there. The way things are, there's nothing the fire brigade can do. There's nothing doing. I'm going back home, just waiting for the opera to catch fire.

— There's no help for it now. That's what happens when brother raises arms against brother.

A gust of wind made a gap in the smoke and people again craned their stiffened necks to watch the fireman with taut hoses and silvery chords of water slipping from their grasp. The crowd had laughing eyes and were reluctant to turn from the scene, when suddenly excitement rustled

** The modernist painter and playwright Witkacy committed suicide three weeks later in fact, when the Russians invaded Poland.

nearby. A little Japanese gent slipped out of the crowd clutching a shiny movie camera; he raised the lens high and stepped back, for the weight was too much and he had trouble keeping his balance. — *Shogun, Shogun* — cries rose from the crowd — you there, *Shogun, sepulu sake san...* And the Japanese gent turned his little face, which was wrinkled like a paradise apple, and bowed to the people. — It's Japanese TV. It'll show the whole truth — the gent nodded rhythmically, — Wałęsa, Wałęsa, — he said to the people standing by him, — Wałęsa, Wawel, Fibak, and they raised their hands with fingers outspread, nodding their heads in agreement, —*Toranaga, toranaga, kilder, ja, ja, guten...*

The Japanese stepped back in fear, as someone grabbed his sleeve and began hectoring him. — We won't surrender, you tell your people, whatever they do, we give them what for, tit for tat it is, and they're not going to win by burning our sanctuaries; and the little fellow retreated into the crowd shielding himself with the long lens of his camera. The man moved doggedly in his tracks, was now poised just above his eardrum, whispering in deep intimacy — They say Pekala's escaped from prison and is getting his own back...

A woman with blurred features was sitting on a scrap of tar-paper on the curb, so stout she might've been dipped in a bladder of opaque fluid; she had a child's plastic piano by her; her swollen fingers fumbled over the keys and she sang, and people tossed coins into an empty cola can propped against the split upper of her gumboot — *Then the screw breaks in the cell, The prisoner he starts to beat, The prisoner falls on his face, And his heart then stops to beat, Then we're all dragged out by night...* — Coins drop into the can and tap out the rhythm, someone tugs at the drunkard plunged in purple dreams on a park bench. — Mister, I say get up mister, you've slept through the best part of it; — That's good. — What's good is it'll stir the conscience of Europe, words can be heard; and for a moment the little drunkard raises his eyelids to reveal white eyeballs, and whispers — Paint me at Calvary...

Things can't be left the way they are, and now a group of former internees has prepared a letter of protest to the authorities. They've collected signatures, but only among themselves. The firemen deploy the ladders and unroll the thin hoses. — Try the other side, try the other side — someone advises them from the crowd, — tackle it from the side and smother the heart of the fire. Smoke enfolds the firemen and absorbs the voice of the crazed man who's shaking his fists at them and spitting pink foam with his words, — Flunkeys, flunkeys...henchmen...

The crowd sways restlessly and turns its back on the conflagration to face a cavalcade of black Tchaikas and Volgas swooping along the roadway. Round faces with puffed and slanted eyes stare morosely ahead, white behind the murky panes; an instant later the raven-black cars vanish beyond the bend, hounded by shouts, jeers and curses.

— We must, I mean, we really must let Wajda know, so he can bring his gear; he can use it afterwards in a film, the National Theatre, today's the March anniversary and you're not telling me it's an accident? a feverish voice is heard and a hand wipes a tear from a cheek. The people around blink, startled by the white light of someone's camera-flash, which poses the flames and smoke against the backdrop of the sky.

A woman holding a squashed hotdog sits on the bench by the drunkard plunged in a malignant fever; grey mushroom sauce trickles onto her knees, but she pays no attention and bites the soggy bread roll and says to the sleeping drunk — I've come from Kielce, spent half the day tramping round town, thinking I'd chance upon the General but I was out of luck, I wanted to so bad, banked on it I did, I've worn my feet out, I deserve a treat, 'cause I've come from Kielce, all the way from Kielce — and he raises an eyelid and gives a sober glance and replies — Yeah, sure, work is for fools, piss-artist rules; mind you, the wops show sex a treat — and his head slowly slips back between the collars of his coat.

From the roof of a neighbouring house a white flock takes flight, swoops above the square, till sucked in by a gust of hot air it spins skywards and vanishes in the thick smoke. The KPN's dropped leaflets — people whisper the news — it's the KPN — the militiamen twitch uneasily, but they're not allowed to shift places, so they frisk the crowd with their eyes, and an old gypsy woman, garishly dressed, threads her way past the cordon and fawns to the idle officials — Hey you, ginger, give us a coin for ripeness, you there, ginger, give us a coin for the belly...

— The Coordination Bureau's already issued a communiqué, somebody here heard from the monitoring — says a man chafing his hands.

The theatre is now thoroughly hobbled with hoses, the firemen climb the ladders like acrobats without holding on, and when they reach the windows they furiously thwack their hatchets at the panes; the dark glass showers the mouldings.

— I'm telling you, the church guard ought'a be called in to restore order. I've got a church guard helmet at home, I could fetch it in just half a sec, couldn't I?

And the firemen, spurred on by the vast eye of the crowd, vanish one after the other in the plush of smoke.

Mauve rays dart from the lights on the car roofs and flit over the motionless faces; eyes brighten then go dim; chilled to the bone, people mechanically stomp their feet — Fancy making someone stand out in this cold. That lot at least are in the warm. It's like an ice-box down here. An ice-box, I tell you.

— The worst thing about it is that truth won't out, as the saying goes. It'll all be hidden from the public eye, as the saying goes.

— Begging your pardon, I don't know what they see in this Marxism of theirs. Not in this Leninism either, begging your pardon.

The National Theatre's ablaze, the crowd remains rooted in the square below and only one man begins to fight his way out of the enclosure; people reluctantly let him pass.

— Where on earth? It's not over yet, where...

— I'm dashing home, it's soon time for the first news on TV. Gotta go. Whatever else, they're bound to show the fire.

Poland Still?

Bells ring above the bulk of the church; swifts swish, black glints against the pargetted wall. Down below, the square expands as a massive crowd pours from the church, then overflows in all directions and stops dead, helpless, sapped of all energy. Darkness rises in the warm breaths, swallows the walls and climbs slowly toward the towers, till the muffled bell dies away.

The crowd is alone.

The crowd is alone and doesn't know what to do with itself, which way to turn, whom to bawl at or what demands to make. It is tired, crumpled and undecided. It's not the-crowd it was, and people eye one another with distrust.

A handful of people like specks of dust break away from the crowd; furtively they unpin the coloured badges on their coats, crowned eagles that could gouge out alien eyes. Compliantly they clench their fingers and nimbly pick their way between the serried ranks of silent militiamen; they dart off to the nearby bus-stops; they just want to lie low at home and forget.

The crowd remains rooted.

People scrutinize one another; not to fall apart, not to disperse, to stay put, stay put; there is after all a chance a settlement could be reached...

— Settle what?

— Well, try and settle all the issues...

— What issues do you mean?

— Well, to discuss...

— Discuss what?

— Well, formulate…

— Formulate what?

— Well, decide everything...

— Decide what?

— Well, coordinate everything...

— But with whom?

— Well, with them…

— With them?

— Not with them…With the others...

— It's high time to coordinate...

— And definitely postulate…

— Absolutely, absolutely…

A husky amplified voice floats out from an undefined point in the dark towards the crowd: — Disperse peacefully, go home, don't form groups, disperse, otherwise we shall have to resort to...

— There's a riot on the way, a man whispers, a riot...

— Time to start?

— Start what?

— Poland Still?*

— Poland Still?

— Well...

— Not yet, not yet...

At a safe distance from here a hunched silhouette cowers behind a windowpane.

— Meduz calling, Meduz calling; it'll probably move, a crowd's formed and now it's waiting, it'll probably move; the blues've lined the square, they're in control; no curses or abuse for the time being, no shouting; right now it's singing *Give us back, O Lord* or something like that, but in patches, in patches; the situation calls for water cannon; when it moves give 'em water cannon for a scare; some of 'em are laughing and gaping, hey, some are already giving the salute and there's our little eye recording it all, and now I can hear *We'll not desert the land* and *You sovietized our kids*; I can see old women and youngsters making the V-sign to one another and laughing; I can see one fellow with a lens recording it all, but it's not one of ours, it's coloured, gaudy as a parrot, he'll be recorded by our lens and he'll have to be checked outside the precincts; the blues are standing quietly by waiting for the kick-off, and then there'll be water for a scare...

*The Polish national anthem begins, *'Poland still has not perished/As long as we are alive.'*

Voices rage more and more distinctly above the crowd, beads of mist settle on bare heads, a helicopter hovers in the darkness and coarsely grinds the dense air.

— Grandpa, a ten-year-old boy asks, say Grandpa, what was it like in Wałęsa's time? In Wałęsa's time, to be perfectly honest — the old man strains his eyes, — well, to tell you the truth it wasn't that simple. There's more than one way. It varied like. One way and the other. That's what. Something like.

And standing aside, the faceless reporter formulates his version for tomorrow morning's news bulletin and asks himself who drove this handful of disoriented youngsters, kids really, to demonstrate; who are the bosses cowering behind the youngsters' backs; who wanted to plant this arsenal of dirty tricks on Polish soil; who lined Geremek's and Michnik's pockets with fat wads of Bonn marks, London pounds, Washington dollars and other foreign currencies; we all know only too well the answers to these and other problems that spring inevitably to the minds of the broad masses of indignant citizens, who in their overwhelming majority daily voice their support. To the disrupters of dialogue and partisans of Star Wars, the spokesmen of national reconciliation resolutely say no. The reporter peers cautiously about him and sees loathsome faces that disgust him. Not long ago he had to repent in sackcloth and ashes before these people, making tearful promises, and he'll never forget his humiliation, never get over that stifling hatred. He fears the crowd and the future.

The collective silence is ominous, and the foreign reporter is also afraid of the crowd; she looks at the crowd, no longer knowing if those faces staring white in the darkness are wild and Asiatic or gentle and wisely European; she is fascinated by the crowd and excited by it; she is in its midst, and at the same time embraces the thousands; she sees two, then four, five and ten thousand; she would hug them to her breast; she ignores the hostile blue lane, for she is a Western reporter; she is untouchable and besides, the communists in Nicaragua did her no harm, she wasn't trampled during the carnival in Havana, so she must get to the bottom of this lot too; thoughts scurry through her brain without her being able to fix on any; a defeat that's not a defeat, a victory that's not a victory, a defeat that'll be a victory, a victory that'll be a victory; she sees an old woman being shunted along by an equally ancient and jaded old boy and hears the woman shouting some words in that strange withered-ivy language that rustles warmly on her parched lips, and the reporter gives the old woman a friendly smile. The other stabs the air with her forked fingers,

— Listen, the woman shouts out, — listen; you think you're badly off, do you? What more do you want? Two televisions each? Three? Did you have those TVs before the war? No, you didn't. Bloody hell!

— Hold it! You right bitch — the man says. — You ain't got a pennyworth of shame...

— Bitch. Bitch. That's all you can say. How many TVs can a man have, when all's said and done?

The edge of the crowd is lined by church guardians in tall caps that look like Uhlan shakos from a distance; the guardians penetrate the crowd; some of them stand motionless and stare at the ZOMO militiamen without a word; and without a word the ZOMO men return the stare.

— Maybe now's the time for Poland Still?

—What?

— Poland Still?

— Poland Still, Poland Still! Not yet...

Voices are borne from end to end of the crowd, which stays put, waiting, not budging an inch; helmets gleam dangerously close, for the time being they hold, stock still as the paving stones; the waiting goes on until from somewhere among the treetops or the church roof muffled words break loose and ripple amid the crowd — What's he saying, what's he saying, that voice; it's the underground speaking on tape, it's a tape; but what's he saying, what's that voice?

<pre>
we shall   we celebrate   not lay down   festival
    we remember   solemnly   as always
  the August   we must   festival   the December
      we'll give   festival   inflexibly   our reply
        achievements   festival   we pledge
      ceremony   our communal   we'll clench
        festival   we persist   we reject
  we recall
        festival   sign our pacts   and postulate
      standing   festival   festive   festival
          celebrat   celebrat   celeb
</pre>

— Well, are we getting on with it, or aren't we? What're we supposed to? people ask the voice, but the voice can't hear; words float through the crowd, the echo lifts them back into the air, into the dark and the mist; the words bounce off the poet; the poet isn't listening, because he's doing his level best to compose a poem that will bear witness, the poet remembers; today the bells are ringing, sounding the alarm, the crowd outside the church, hope kindled in its hearts, while the red dragon in the sky flaps its real tail in vain, in vain it sends its cohorts in; and the poet pauses awhile as the rhyme for cohorts eludes him, what rhymes with cohorts? Cohorts, reports; janissaries, mercenaries; but Poland still has to be fitted in, phalanx black hundreds tatars mortars, there's still nothing to rhyme with Poland... so the poet leaves the rhyme for later, and for the time being constructs a couplet, repeating the words with emphasis for fear they may give him the slip:

Rejoice not, vicious dragon red;
The day we fight, you'll soon be dead...

— Well folks, what are we doing? someone asks in an unnaturally loud voice — Seeing as we're doing nothing,we'd better be snappy. The guardians in the chef's-hat helmets stalk the crowd with their eyes; people retreat respectfully just in case; they exchange swift glances and slight motions of the head; the man over there is silent beyond recall and someone else, wanting to smooth over the situation, explains coaxingly: — I might even get the truncheon. Better still. Let England know. Then we'll see. England must say stop. Either there's some justice in the world, or there isn't.

A woman squeezes her way deftly through the crowd; she is wearing trousers and a blue sweater and a too-small cap with a pompom on a thread that bobs about like a yoyo; she peers into the bystanders' eyes and whispers — Buy Hungar fruit drops, Hungar bubblegum, what, fruit drops, fruit drops...

— Wouldn't mind some of the bubble stuff, but it depends how much — someone mutters mechanically, but he makes no move and the woman's voice drifts into the distance and a child tugs hopefully at its mother's sleeve, and she says without looking, in a tone of torment — Get off my sleeve, get off my sleeve, or I'll knock you off.

— So what's up?

— How d'you mean what's up?

— When's the speech?

— It's already been.

— How come? When?

— Why ask? Ought've listened ...

— When was the speech?

— Wakey wakey — the man unexpectedly replies, and looking round in triumph, he breaks out into prolonged uncontrollable laughter that blocks his windpipe.

— Must be time for Poland Still?

—What?

— How about Poland Still?

— Poland Still... Not yet...

The foreign television team probes the crowd with its lens. A correspondent swathed in a coloured scarf adopts a professional air and hassles the cameraman for good measure. Make sure you show the church helping Solidarity. It's a must.

— I know my job.

— It must be made clear. When you did the prison, you were meant to show the political prisoners. And all you could see was walls, bare walls. Nothing to show it was political. Just bars and rooftops.

— I did it myself — says the cameraman, offended.

— There's nothing to get uptight about — the correspondent says. — If you did it, then that's OK. Can you see how the church is being supportive?

— Clear as day.

— Well then, we'll be off.

— Couldn't we perhaps wait for the bloodshed?

— Bloodshed, ah, bloodshed. The trouble with bloodshed...

The crowd waits patiently; shouts and scraps of songs sparkle in the darkness; words reverberate against the plastic shields of the impenetrable militia.

Again the loudspeaker is heard from the roof of a car slowly driving round the posts and cordons.

— I appeal to you to disperse.

— By the church they can't touch us.

— They won't enter the precincts. We're immune.

— Not here they won't. Out there it's different.

— Out there they would.

The crowd is rooted but will probably soon move under the batons, it has no other way out.

Here and there banners open like flowers.

The crowd stirs, no one asks where, it won't get far anyway.

The crowd knows it will be routed and will achieve nothing.

But it sallies forth because it has no other way of honouring today's anniversary. So the crowd celebrates the way it knows best.

A stone's throw from here asylum ends at the black asphalt and the rasping loudspeaker on the car roof. There's a cordon ahead waiting to receive the crowd.

Faces are now turned in the opposite direction, rage and despair and fear swell in the helpless people, mouths are rent by more and more cries.

— Flunkeys!
— Gestapo!
— Bandits!
— Scroungers!
— Fascists!
— Anti-Poles!
— Red plague!
— Butchers!
— Renegades!

The disciplined ranks give a faint shudder, but do not stir from their posts. The transparent visors drop with a clatter and a glassy wall of shields rears up.

The crowd waves, sways, swells.

And suddenly the first drops fall, followed by an abundant rain of coins; the crowd chucks fistfuls of small change at the motionless ranks; the coins glitter in the lamplight like a shoal of fish on the move.

The ranks withdraw not a step; the rain slowly abates, the crowd soon runs out of loose change; people breathe helplessly and watch...

Single huddled silhouettes break away from the crowd; their numbers increase as people watch speechless; they stoop dutifully before the cordon; they are within the batons' reach; they crouch low and eagerly scoop up the coins and stuff them into their pockets; elderly fingers fumble feverishly in the mud.

— Disperse singly to your homes! — cries the loudspeaker on the car roof.

Brightened by the falling coins, the darkness slowly fades.

— Friends, look friends, how could you...

— Why ask, why ask...You'll be old too one day. And you'll just have a pension to live on. Then you'll see. Just you wait...

— You have to make ends meet somehow...

Pockets stuffed, indifferent, the pensioners carry their booty into the crowd.

—Now?

—What now?

— Poland Still?

— Poland Still? Any minute now.

The crowd stirs.

VICTO...

That day was just like any other, it washed the clotted square as before; people dodged between the cars towards the bus stops, wedged their way into shops and huddled round the ice-coated window of the commissary with its transistor radio and gleaming asiatic teaspoons; where the window-dresser had thrown in a snakeskin and some cotton shirts with purple hearts and English wording *I love New York, I love London, Smile, Kiss Me*; people fought silently for vantage points to gape at the objects, and a child whispered beseechingly to its father — Oh let's go now, let's go and have a look at the hard currency stores; the nearest ones are in Graniczna Street, in Stawki, Intrako, in Piwna Street and there's one in the Hotel Europe, just two stops away; and tomorrow we can still go to Jerusalem Avenue, the Forum and the Polonia...

A frozen vendor in a pointed cap made of newspaper stood motionless by his soda-water dispenser; the slogan *Proletarians of the World* ran across his forehead only to vanish behind his ear, and a raspberry icicle the size of a stalactite hung from the dispenser tap; the vendor thrummed it thoughtfully like a harp string... He appeared to be dozing with his head askew and muttering in his sleep; he was in fact squinting at the polished surface of the dispenser, in which his newspaper cap and the newsprint were reflected, and he slowly mouthed the words that were reflected backwards as in a mirror and which he read in reverse...six small elephants — donated — by Cuba — arrived — in a temperature — of minus thirty — at Moscow Zoo. They sailed — to Leningrad — wrapped — in warm — woolly blankets. — They travelled from — Leningrad — to — Moscow — in — specially — heated — railway — coaches — and — from — Moscow — station — to — the — zoo— in heated — cars. They arrived in fine form...

He tugged nervously on the raspberry icicle and it fell with a clang onto the wording reflected on the table-top, crossing it through with a red line... — Mother-fucker, oh, mother-fucker — the vendor whispered white-mouthed, and the day drifted and wavered above the square and dragged in its wake days and months and years to come...

No one knew when it happened; in a split second white caps sprouted at the exit of the square, countless whistles tore the day and blocked the way to cars; nimble white wristbands waved them impatiently off, people slipped warily away; a bus slowly rolled into a side street, and the bewildered passengers, whisked off in an unknown direction, flung mute curses from behind glass and helplessly shook their fists...

As though struck unawares by a gust of wind the square emptied quickly, silence fell upon silence, militiamen appeared so suddenly they might've stepped out from the plasterwork, they surrounded the square, sauntering about with feigned nonchalance, a bunch of people who had nowhere to hide stayed put on the bus stop island, they continued standing there and really couldn't care and didn't even look up to see what had disrupted their day; nearby a lopsided taxi dug into the ground, it couldn't be hauled from the square as it had only three wheels to stand on, the fourth wheel lay alongside the chassis. The bewildered taxi driver stared at it and stooped and gently fingered it, then straightened up again and kicked it with rage, and a breathless woman ran across the empty square; with the last remnant of her strength she ran up to the taxi and tugged at the door; the three-wheeled vehicle keeled like a boat; the driver gazed at the crowd for a long while, then said, — If that was a man, he'd be no more than a heap of rubble now... but as things are... — and he dropped on his knees by the wheel and froze in that posture.

A green bus entered from a side street, came to a halt and began to churn out soldiers with musical instruments; the leader shouted protracted orders, and his barge-hauler's voice gave shape to the amorphous mass; an instant later there were no more people; a squad of four stood to attention in the square and upon imbibing the last command it lurched forward and set off toward the middle of the empty square, where there were stone steps and a plinth bearing a gigantic figure with a metal cloak covered in greenish patina and clutching a metal book in its metallic right palm...* The four soldiers marched up to the figure without slowing their pace and had it not been for the sudden command that stopped it in its tracks, it might even have overturned that metallic giant...

A militiaman stood motionless surveying the people on the island, waited, and failed to see his uniformed colleague steal up behind him; he crept closer and closer, then pounced, landed him a mighty thump and like an eagle-owl hooted down his eardrum boo-oo; the militiaman leaped about, his first reflex was to grab his cap for fear of losing it, and grip his baton and pistol, only to freeze in his tracks; his colleague eyed him condescendingly, nodded his head and barked — What, 'fraid of the militia, mate? — and gave such a laugh that a passenger at the bus stop shuddered as though wrenched out of a dream...

The military band froze; wind, frost and dust dulled the golden glints of the musical instruments, and at the bus stop people stood, not even wondering how long they would have to wait; they stood because they had taken up positions; the place was no worse than any other, no one was kicking them out. And so they stood.

Women held their heads confidentially close: — And so I tells him he's not to speak to me like that, so he tells me not to tell him, so I tells him to belt up. — You mean to say you said that to him? What did he say to that? The taxi driver jacked up the car and was helplessly fitting the wheel, which kept falling away

— Know the one about children and the windshield wipers? — a voice piped up, — children and windshield wipers...

— Windshield wipers?

— Right. Turn on the windshield wipers when the brakes fail.

— What? What the devil?

— You know, mister. The blood. To scrape the guts from the glass. And the blood.

— Don't you try telling me that bullshit.

— Haven't much sense of humour, have we? None whatsoever. — the voice sounds offended, then falls silent.

People blinked as flashing blue lights wreathed the square, lights that danced along the house walls only to fade in midair in a perfect siberia of clouds; a cavalcade of gleaming Mercedes and Volgas and Tchaikas and Ladas slipped soundlessly into the square; chauffeurs in smart caps leaped out and obligingly opened doors; the square buzzed and blushed with bright-coloured wreaths; in the wink of an eye the newcomers lined up, each perfectly in place; the line stood at ease, fidgeted momentarily, then froze in position; the display was spoiled by the somewhat protruding figure of a black man shivering so violently from cold that he kept jerking about; but the rank promptly drew him in and order was resumed; the rank froze, stood to attention and music blared from the band; the taxi driver didn't so much as glance in its direction.

— There'll be special deliveries to the shops, I'll bet.

— What a hope. Not for the likes of that. Not a ghost of a chance ...

— For the Revolution they will, with luck.

— Not for the Revolution they won't. More likely for Rebirth...if anything.

— Rebirth's more than six months to go. But it's a dead cert. They can't fail to, not for Rebirth they can't.

— And if they don't, so what? Fuckin' great mongrel.

The music swayed above the square, and the first three-some clutching a wreath stepped out of the row heading for the greenish metal figure as drums rolled like dried peas underfoot; a soldier led them like blind men though the three pairs of slanting eyes knew the way full well; finally they halted, two soldiers received the wreath, worried over it at the foot of the plinth, and the red-tongued sashes blew about in the wind; the wreath at last settled, the soldiers stood to attention, the threesome stood awhile apparently counting to ten, then together bowed its three heads before the plinth and walked back to take up positions at the end of the line, and from the front the next threesome was already stepping out to a drum-roll.

— When all's said and done, he's a Pole like the rest of us. I mean look at his surname, never mind about his first name.

— If he's a Pole, then I'm not.

— What do you mean, you're not a Pole?

— I mean just what I say, see.

— Then who the hell are you? A Turk? A ruddy Turk?

— I'd rather be a Turk any day than that.

— Pole or no Pole — the bus stop chipped in — when it comes to it they'll make him into a Sienkiewicz. But first they'll have to stick a few more books under his armpits.

The would-be taxi passenger stood forever motionless, then raised her head and noticed the row of neatly parked

Mercedes and Volgas and Tchaikas and Ladas at the far end of the square; she glanced covetously at the row of cars and darted off across the square, banking on easy prey, a small and lonely figure; but two large silhouettes loomed by her side, she gesticulated, pointed toward the cars, waved some coloured banknotes, then headed toward the bus stop for shelter.

— She was lucky to be let off, if she'd gone any further she'd be no more than a heap of rubble — said the taxi driver, his blue fingers tightening a nut.

The next threesome counted to ten and gave a triple-headed bow to the statue, but its metal head paid no attention and its greenish eyes peered sideways somewhere above the square. The stack of wreaths grew, the wind braided the ribbons and exotic inscriptions, mingling alphabets and languages across frontiers.

— I'm in such a bad way — someone in the queue was complaining — ever so bad — can you imagine, my TV's broken and I ain't got a clue what's going on, like a moth banging my head against the wall.

— Mmmmm, and there's ever such good things on...

— Well I never, I can't wait to hear...

— Mmmmm, all sorts of stuff like, a guy came from Koscierzyna and did his impersonation of a trumpet, and another guy did a belly dance and tied two feet of thread into two hundred and fifty knots, and there was a guy who played a tune with his nails on his teeth, and a couple that's real popular right now, a brother and sister, duet for two jaws, mmmmmm, and a poetess in overalls from a village near Siedlce sang a pig-song of her own composition, and in the program on carp-breeding the carp at the end said merry Christmas, and then the news bulletin said a lot of passengers had flown into Okecie and couldn't remove their fur coats, mmmmmm, and they turned out to be foxes and the lopsided woman reporter held the mike up to the cage and said good day mr fox, how are you today, what, can't you unbutton yourself, what, he was mute as a fish...mmm-mmm...

— My old man after all that has connected the TV to the radio and now we watch the box on the radio, and they said there's sex in the sideboard and jangling forks, to which the women said good but only so-so, and oh what a hoot, eight hours the family waited with the stiff, people came from all over Poland, well and then what, no coffin to be had, no coffin for love or money, and then that Wałęsa stabbed the nation in the back, oh it's a sorry state, a sorry, sorry state...

Three heads demurely bowed to the metal boots, yes, yes, yes, they appeared to be reiterating their undying oath, unsure whether the metal figure would altogether trust them.

Then drums rolled once again and the next threesome carried its wreath like a shield against the venomous wind, but the people at the bus stop did not so much as glance in their direction; they were listening to the woman who woke up with a smile in a corner of the shelter and set eyes on two silent males and was saying to them with gentle persuasion, hey boys, want to have some fun? I've got two daughters, nine and seven, let's have a giggle. I live just across the road, only came out for a breath of fresh air, come on lads, I promise you won't regret it...

The eyes of the previous threesomes rested on the last triplet and its wreath; it was a delegation of Polish youth; it stepped out to the drums, two boys and a girl carrying the wreath, all in chequered trousers; the metal figure on the plinth lured them like a magnet; when they approached, the soldier escorting them walked away; two other soldiers received the coloured wreath from the girl and placed it with some difficulty in the remaining space at the figure's feet; then they stood to attention, and the threesome counted to ten; the girl prompted herself by imperceptibly tapping out the rhythm, then at last the three young heads bowed simultaneously as though to check if they had clean shoes, and the girl's blond hair blew over her forehead and screened her cheeks; the line-up beamed with pride and content at the representatives of Polish youth, and the girl felt the touch of their glances and her cheeks blushed as they stepped lightly past the line-up, borne on the eyes of the onlookers; once they were back in their places, the girl sighed and blew the hair from her cheek, then glanced at her companions and licked her parched lips with the tip of her tongue...

And the band struck again at the sky, and the line-up stood tense as though with cramp and listened earnestly to the song; then order broke, people made a beeline for the cars, doors slammed and violet lights flashed on the roofs and the cavalcade drove off; the woman running toward the taxi recovered her wits, spotted the cars and began to wave her arm rhythmically, stooping down to the curb; the Mercedes, Volgas, Tchaikas and Ladas sailed by, but she kept on waving her hand; the musicians put away their mouthpieces and shook the saliva from the brass...

And the white caps that had barred the entrance to the square vanished, cars and buses reappeared and in a trice the square was full of people; the scene drifted away like a dream, and only the coloured wreaths lay stacked at the foot of the towering figure...

The taxi driver flung the jack into the car, slammed the lid to no effect, then flapped his hand in resignation and pulled the tail of his jacket from under his duffel and slowly wiped his greasy fingers.

A bus drew up at the stop and those getting off jammed into those getting on; the jittery driver didn't even notice he had lit the filter of his fag and framed his passengers in the wings of his pneumatic doors...

— I could take you in a pinch — the taxi driver said to the woman standing in a daze by the curbside — but only as far as Wola, 'cause I'd make nothing on it; but if we went by Gorczewska Street we could clock up another couple of kilometers, 'cause I've got a cousin who's got the dropsy, that's worth a look in...

The last militiamen and civilians dispersed from the foot of the monument into the crowd.

A man in a short sheepskin jacket appeared at the bus shelter, extracted a brush from an inside pocket, and on the armoured glass drew large letters that began to shape the word VIC...

The subdued square came alive, people strained their eyes to the point of tears in search of their bus numbers, no one paid attention to the weary provocateur writing on glass. Only the last cop gave him a discreet wink from beneath his visor as he strolled past, gestured faintly with his hand, jerked his chin at the indifferent people and gave a mild shrug of the shoulders...

VICTO...

*Editor's note –the unidentified statue in this story seems to be a memorial to a political figure or writer promoted by the communist regime, but many communist era statues have now been moved, and squares like the former Victory Square in Warsaw have been renamed.

The Three Kings

The netting, rusty as lichen, bars the assembled people from the garden allotments.

Scorched by the night frost, clusters of limp tulips hang from the net, and a faded icon sways in the gusts of wind. Behind the netting lonely figures of allotment owners stoop and poke about among last year's overgrowth of weeds; dust rises from clumps of dry stalks at every touch.

Bent to the ground, they occasionally glance at those on the other side of the netting lest anyone try to slip through to their patches. And they ponder the sky and cover the seedbeds with wrapping paper to protect the soil from the radioactive dust*; they secure the sheets with stones, but the eastern wind delivers its dispatches everywhere.

The slanting walls of glasshouses lie between the people and the town, which resounds today with marching music and bustles like an Asiatic bazaar.

Those on the other side of the netting stand in a tight huddle; women whisper among themselves and point their fingers and tighten their kerchief knots under their chins;

*This story coincides with the Chernobyl nuclear disaster in spring 1986.

solemn men stand on one side, shielding lit cigarettes in their cupped palms; they exhale an odour of days-old alcohol and insomnia.

— I saw it as sure as I see you.

— You say you saw it?

— That's what I'm telling you. And I can see it now.

— What, in colour?

— In technicolour. Sure as I stand here.

— Sort of rainbow-like?

— What're you driving at? — the woman was perturbed.

— Nothing. Just asking.

— You mean you can see it too?

— No, no, I can't see a thing. I'm only asking if it's rainbow-like.

—Yes, like a rainbow. What d'ya mean? — the woman asks suspiciously. — Can you see something too?

— Not a sausage. And my eyeballs is aching. But nothing doing.

— So now you see.

The people stand rooted in the trampled meadow pitted with mole-hills. The wind inflates the printed papers clinging to the wire.

Behind the wire stretches a row of patches and sheds, botched together from bits of crates, planks and tar paper. — *Bucher aus Polen* (Books from Poland) — people mouth the inscriptions on the walls.

— That German *bicher* is good stuff — they say approvingly. It's good stuff, that German *bicher*, waterproof. Someone brought a crate of it back from a trip. It lasts a good couple of years, too.

— Maybe if it's not burned out by the russki atom — they nod and tilt their heads so as to scrutinize the sheds more professionally.

The allotments are adjacent to the brick wall of the cemetery, above which trees spread out their black boughs. People anxiously search the branches with their eyes — See, where they sort of fork off, that's where it is; there, see, more to the side, by those branches; I can see a blue mantle. Over that shed over there with the *Veritas* on the wall. That's where I can see it.

Far away, three old men stand at a curb, separated from the sidewalk opposite by a lively procession swelling the full width of the roadway; the other side is out of reach, yet they must somehow cross it on their way to the suburbs and the allotments next to the wall of swollen red bricks.

Women in coloured aprons dart along the roadway, their heads immersed in moth ball fumes; hemmed in by a ring of glum men in lacquered boots, they all execute some sort of dance, but the band has not yet struck up and the cavalcade proceeds in a silent void, except for the crackling of puffy breeches and stiff petticoats. — Here come the good folk of Siedlce — the loudspeakers roar overhead — nimble-toed as ever, Siedlce. — Men whose two-day stubble creeps up to their bloodshot eyes sullenly cut capers and spin their scared womenfolk round in a fury.

— Buses aren't working today — the three men say.

— We'll never get to the miracle on foot.

— The trams will be coming on later. But we gotta get across. Gotta get to the Vistula.

— Not a chance. They're not letting people through — says the old man with a sun-blackened face.

— How long can the procession last?

— Ages. They go on and on. I must be seeing double, but that's the third time those soldiers have gone by.

— Those women in the aprons have been past once already.

— Not this lot. That was the Lomza contingent. They had aprons too; easy to confuse.

— We'll never make it on time, if this goes on another couple of hours it'll be night.

People stare through the wire mesh at the tree-tops and wait in hope, envying those who have seen and in a feverish exchange of details confirm it was no hallucination.

— A single figure, just by itself.

— Not at all, it was a large, bright-coloured head.

— What head? What are you going on about?

— A head I said. Coloured.

— But a head can't appear by itself.

— Why on earth not?

— Because it can't.

— But it can if it wants. A head can appear by itself if it wants to.

— I tell you it's impossible. It must be full-length.

— But where is it?

— See where the branches form a sort of shelter? It's quite distinct. It's even moving.

— But not there. Your marbles must've come loose.

From the wall of the glasshouses people stream across the meadow; at the sight of the crowd by the wire they quicken their pace, women run, cleaving the air with their bags, and shamefaced smiles fade, full of incredulity. The crowd grows...

— Perhaps we might make a dash for it — the old boys think out loud. — When there's an intermission.

— Dash where? We'll be trampled to dust. Not so much as noticed. The procession has eyes only for itself... If only...

Several sweaty men steal away from the procession clutching a gigantic balloon on a rope; it soars overhead, and the men exchange feverish whispers, wipe their faces and glance on all sides; then one of them speaks to the old fellows.

— You wouldn't mind holding the balloon, comrades? Eh? For just a mo? 'Cause we've got business to do... And the balloon has to...before the stand. You'll take the rope, won't you, comrades? — a purple man asks with wily hope and at one tug opens the shirt on his swollen neck.

The old men eye one another in panic.

— How long for?

— Only a mo, and...

— And you'll come and collect it? — the old fellow enquires suspiciously.

— I should think so. We signed a chit for it. Have to hand it back after theprocession. It's been parading past the tribune for years. At the head, in the middle, a sort of symbol like. In Gierek's day, too, only it went a different route, maybe you remember. Way back in Wieslaw's day even. So you'll take it, eh?

— Just thinking...it won't blow away?

— Not likely. It's half full. Bye-bye then — the man brightens up. —There's nothing like a Pole to give a 'elping 'and.

The old men fumble at the rope, the balloon sways to a wave of a military march — Hey mister — the old man calls, but they're cut off from the crowd by a huge wing of red material that flaps about their legs and arms, and when the wind dispels the red haze, the other fellows have gone, vanished into the bowels of the earth.

The balloon hovers docilely overhead, the rope flags and they can handle it easily. The balloon slowly revolves and the old boys, laboriously craning their heads, decipher the inscription at its base: *Warm Welcome to the Congress...*

An old woman holds her oil-cloth bag to her left ear to shield it from the needling wind and gazes, eyes teared, at the allotment sheds, the cemetery wall and the trees beyond, and turns back helplessly to the crowd.

— There's no figure there at all, nothing.

— Nothing? — people are bewildered and incredulous.

— Nothing whatsoever. I can't see anything.

— How can there be nothing when they showed it on TV and we saw it? We did.

— TV, oh well, TV. They may've seen a vision. But it's not appearing to me.

— But it's got to — they reassure the disappointed woman.

— Maybe all this atomic wind has blurred it.

The crowd swells, newcomers fidget uneasily — Where's that miracle — they ask. — Over there, above the shed, in the mantle — local men in threadbare jackets with upturned collars patiently explain.

— Now what do we do with this balloon? — the old men ask in dismay. — Those comrades've gone. Gone with the wind.

— Maybe they'll come back. They said they'd signed...signed a chit...

— They won't come back. They've palmed the balloon off on us.

— I mean we can't take it to the allotments...

— Or get on the tram with it...

— Dump it on someone?

— Who would want it?

They are drowned by the loud menacing words of the song and the shouts of a reporter battling his way through the noise; a disorderly crowd of schoolchildren in trade school caps trails along the street, encircled by a ring of teachers who keep standing on tiptoe and craning their necks to keep count of them; several pupils evade their watchful glances and draw up on the curb; they huddle in apparent consultation, and with nimble fingers they roll up the canvas on the flagstaffs they'd been hoisting; then with the tips of the red-cocooned rods they grope for the sewer manhole and quickly shove them down, and step back onto the sidewalk; the banners disappear down the sewer like floats, and the pupils cower and evade the experienced eye of their tutors.

— Get us Free Europe — one of them says — there may be a bulletin about the nuclear cloud...

His mate pulls out a small transistor radio and scans the wave band, catches voices amid the crackles, and they bend their heads over the receiver and hear a woman and a man, and their ravelled words, — There's one solution for loneliness in a woman's life — says the man— it's to become a councilor. A councilor can go to a café with her councilor colleague and there's no gossiping.

— Idiot, that can't be Free Europe — say the disappointed pupils, so the owner of the radio perseveres at the knob and finally gets a report on the procession; a gust of wind tugs at the balloon and the old men dig their fingers into the slippery cord for all they're worth ...

— So I saw another figure, slightly to the side. Over that shed, right. Golden rays. Chestnut hair just like yours — and the informant tugs at the hair of the woman standing by her — shoulder-length chestnut hair — she thumps her in the shoulder blades — about so long. With a beard. Sad-faced. Seemed ready for the worst. Seemed to know what was brewing. Oh, and the gold rays, but I told you that already.

— That's more or less what I saw. A full-length figure standing in the branches. Gave me quite a turn because ...

— Oh, I wouldn't swear to it. In the evening I'd see better. But I'm blind as a bat by day. Could be seeing things ...

— I can see it moving. This way, that way ...

And the inhabitants of the glasshouse stand at the windows with their binoculars aimed alternately at the clump of trees beyond the cemetery wall and at the sky, from which the invisible dust quietly falls.

— Ah, the veterans with the balloon — a woman rushes up to the old men, her coat flying in the wind, and eyes them soberly.

— Come for the balloon? — they hopefully ask. — Here you are. All in one piece.

— Get lost with that balloon — the woman gets excited.

— We must make an announcement over the radio, issue hourly communiqués about the peace conference to be convened the day after tomorrow. It must be convened in the Column Hall of Parliament. We must summon a committee immediately to broadcast communiqués every hour about the conference in the Column Hall. I can't get that committee to work.

The old men gaze at the woman in bewilderment and, still holding the rope, tuck their hands behind their backs.

— Yesterday I spoke with a group from Cuba. Very understanding they were. Very sympathetic. The Column Hall of Parliament, then. And you'll join the committee. As veterans.

— But the militia'll rout us — one old man hesitantly says.

— So you're afraid of the militia?

— I sure am — the old man says sincerely.

— Well, I'm not. And I'm a woman.

— Because you don't know life, missy. Besides, we haven't got time. We've got to get to Praga. To the allotments.

— Where will it get you, all this running around in circles? There and back. I'm going to the hotels now. There's three hotels in all. I need to find the delegation from Cuba. They'll take part in the peace conference in the Column Hall in Parliament. They promised me. Very decent people. Gave me wholehearted support. And you must sign the declaration.

— I'm not going to sign anything — says the old man, tugging at the rope.

— Well, you might at least have a spot of iodine (to protect against the radiation)? — the woman enquires, and without waiting for a reply, she makes a beeline for a group of steelworkers walking along the roadway in ceremonial costumes.

— My eyes are hanging out and nothing to show for it — says the woman, who turns away disappointedly from the netting, wipes the stains of rust from her fingers and grabs a strand of grey hair of the woman standing next to her.

— My, but you do have light hair. Beautiful — She fingers the head of the motionless woman and pulls back her ears. — So light and fine. I had a jar of lemon for a couple of years for washing mine, but it fell out all the same. Yours is pretty. The thing is to add spirits to the egg yolk, otherwise it congeals and clogs up the hair. But it's too late now. It'll drop out after that cloud like anything. And we'll all go on the same hearse when we go.

— But I did see it — the woman protests in desperate defense. — Besides, if you believe, you don't have to see, you just believe you see...

— Maybe, maybe not — a pensive voice replies. — Folks these days are suspicious anyway. In the old days they'd lie flat on the ground for a miracle. They don't even know what they want nowadays.

— That's 'cause they can't figure out the sense of things no more — others say soothingly and turn round again in the opposite direction, only to face the brick wall.

— That'll be the thirteenth miracle since the war — one of the old men shouts above the brass band. — The balloon's beginning to make my hands ache.

— Thirteenth. That could bring them bad luck — the second jerks his chin somewhere to the side.

— Thirteenth, that's right. In 'forty-nine it was in Lublin, in 'fifty-seven in Kossak Square in Kraków, in 'fifty-eight in Chełmek... — the third starts counting.

— In 'fifty-nine the tower was alight in Muranów, what had been painted over — says the second.

— In 'sixty-five a girl in Zabłudów saw a miracle. So her mother was arrested for spreading false news ... — the third expounds.

— In 'seventy-one near Radzymin, then in 'seventy-four in Piotrków Kujawski, and in 'seventy-five in Wrocław.

— 'Eighty-one in Olecko.

— 'Eighty-four in Oława.

— 'Eighty-four in Karczew, too.

— A regular rainfall of miracles over the last few years.

— And what's more, we always used to get there on time. But with this balloon...

A crocodile of white-bonneted nurses proceeds along the highway. The young women glance about them, fidget behind the backs of their friends and break out in nervous, uncontrollable laughter...

And every few steps, at the command of the sister-in-charge, the line alters its pace, gives a hop and a skip as if it had hiccoughs.

A young man sidles up to the three old men, his hand hidden significantly beneath his left armpit; he gives them a professional look-over, then whispers to the one nearest him — Pair of tights for the missis? — and he rustles cellophane beneath his jacket.

— Has anyone seen the miracle? — people press together, averting weary eyes from the cemetery wall.

— What do you mean, has anyone? Everybody's seen the miracle.

— I've even got a snapshot.

— Then let's see it, madam.

— I haven't got it on me, it's at my sister's. It's in colour.

— Then show us, missis, if that's the case.

— I haven't got it on me, I tell you. It's at my sister's.

Close up you can't tell how to hold it. But from a distance you can. You have to take your hand away to see. All colours. Pink and blue.

— Maybe you're pulling my leg...

Offended, the woman turns away and shrugs.

— Say what you like, but a miracle's nothing to scoff at.

A sickly vapour rises above the meadow, people's eyes water. Nauseating kitchen smells come from the concrete wall of the house, as well as the amplified boom of the procession on TV.

The local cop, clutching his satchel in his leather glove, wades through the meadow towards the crowd; the martial music from the procession drives his reluctant pace forward.

And so he reaches the wall of human shoulders, pauses indecisively and opens his mouth to speak, then claps it shut and rushes toward a molehill, burrows with the tip of his boot, crouches, stretches out his hand and straightens up again.

He grasps a dirty pen in his hand, shakes off the lumps of soil, peers round, blows on the ballpoint and positions his left hand to test it, promptly pulls off his leather glove and begins to draw some sprawling characters. He stares at his hand and enunciates, as though reading a bulletin.

— Come on, folks. What's the point of gathering here? Disperse and go home. 'Cause there'll be trouble.

People standing nearby turn round and see the lonely cop facing them; they look at him without fear.

—Come on, folks. There's nothing there. There never was. Not since I came on duty — the constable says hesitantly, his eyes fixed on his left hand. — I mean there's no apparition, nothing...

— Miracles don't appear to sinners — says a voice from the crowd.

— Or the unworthy.

Silence falls, then voices rise again with growing certitude; people exchange astonished looks as though they had made some unexpected discovery.

— Far more useful if you ask me. The worthy don't need it. But the unworthy might be converted...

— Come on, folks, disperse. Don't cause an obstruction. Miracles don't come on tap — he says without conviction, staring at the cluster of trees above the wall...

The old men feel their hands go weak; gusts of wind and music tug the balloon in all directions.

One of them extracts a packet of Populars from his pocket and shoves it toward his companions, and they help themselves with their free hands, then stoop over the slender match flames. Unawares, they let the rope slip from their stiff fingers, and the balloon bounds up into the air, then sideways. A group of small girls with drums strapped to their bellies stop waving their sticks, their wide eyes following its unsteady flight. The wind twists the balloon and hurls it against the banners hoisted on high rods by two railway workers from the junction; the surface rips on the sharp end of one of the rods; it emits a whirring stream of gas and tears the second slogan from the railway workers' hands, *Our Railwaymen Say No to American Nuclear Rockets,* and the balloon tosses madly, causing havoc among the marchers.

Women squeal as they yank their motley dresses; the railwaymen press their caps to their heads and pick up the bent cardboard letters from the asphalt; and the flabby balloon flounders on the pavement like a jellyfish.

Suddenly there's a crowd of youths milling about the three terrified old men, hemming them in, grabbing them tight by the arms; several bellicose commands in fragments assail them: disruption of proceedings, sabotage of ceremony; but they can't understand what has happened and look round helplessly and don't know why they are being frog-marched towards a grey police van.

— We must get to the allotments — one of them tries to say, then falls silent.

— You'll be getting your allotments — they hear a jeering voice. — Everybody'll get their allotment.

And when they stand outside the open door of the van and look up, they start to say that the step is too high, but all they hear is the snap of words:

— Hey, you three kings, hop into the disco...

Chain of Pure Hearts

The pair of them stood silently facing each other; not a word; then they hunched, squatted and began simultaneously to retreat, jostling people indifferently; they looked like two dwarfs readying for a duel, and the red folds they were unfurling over the ground grew longer and longer between them till they couldn't take half a step more on this leash, so they straightened up; they held the ends of the material, peered at the letters in yellow glitter, and attempted to flick off the remnants of old slogans, but the glue gave way and the slogan surged overhead for a moment; they jerked their heads in amazement and even had time to read it; *Come Sun, Come Rain, Come Join the Chain*; the wind struck and the letters gyrated like little albatrosses; the layout began to disintegrate; first the slogan lost its meaning, then the words; the wind whipped up again and carried the loose letters and dashed them against the black bosom of the stone giantess propping her shoulders against the wall of the Palace of Culture.

The pair of them observed the flight of the slogan, letters, words; and then as the white scraps scattered on the stone lady's lap and feet, they shrugged their shoulders, turned about toward the van, selected the next roll of cloth and again started moving backwards on their haunches, as though they were hunting for fag-ends among the cracks of the granite flagstones. A white slogan bloomed: *Don't Miss the Boat, Go and Vote*! They mouthed syllables amid the scraping and clatter of numerous feet, shrugged their shoulders, wound the material up, carried it back to the van, found another roll and without a word began walking backwards in the shadow of Stalin's pyramid.

People were gathering in the square, watching the television team entangle itself in cables, the lackadaisical reporters and cameramen with their equipment, a small purple man in a cyclist's cap cramming words into a mike. He stood in an open car and tense assistants busied over him as they recorded his speech; he kept straying from the mike and signaling; the assistants would rewind the tape and play it back; he listened keenly, turned more and more purple, then grabbed back the mike, glancing at a wad of index cards. — A magnificent concern, integration, let us defend, the idea of love, we shall be the first in our country, to be victorious, love, love, dearly beloved, for we'll always be together, elderly, let's join hands young and old alike, chain, to love, love, let's all clasp hands and we shall stand, the way of truth,our chain shall unite the land, our honesty sincerity success joy happiness, my, our, we'll be together, our common road, understanding, common life, ours, to love, love, chain, the whole country, to embrace, understanding, to embrace, join hands, everyone, everyone, to love — and he heard these words again, pressing the mike to his cyclist's cap, and in the increasing hubbub the pair of them unfurled the next slogan and read it with cocked heads and shrugged their shoulders: *The Chain Belongs to All of Us, Without It, You're Not One of Us.*

The first drops of rain cut through the air and died in a hiss on the cracked flagstones; a reporter took a plastic bag from under his arm, removed two sandwiches from it, stuffed the bread into his pocket and with an awkward movement of one hand attempted to pull the bag over his head to protect his hair; scratching his skull, he sauntered up to a group of people standing quietly to the side clasping hands.

— The chain? Are you the chain? — he casually asked.

— The chain of pure hearts! — they replied, and he looked like a conductor as he caught voices from various angles with deft movements of the mike.

— We've waited a long time for an initiative of this sort. And now the chain has been launched at last, it will unite us from the mountains to the sea, it will be a milestone on the way to national conciliation, a powerful protest against the cosmic spiral of cowboy... — and the reporter nodded his head in time and chewed his rain-sodden bread, and when he switched off the mike, the others let go their hands and clustered round him. — Will it be on the radio, will it be broadcast? — I should say it will — he replied, munching his bread. A savvy sort of girl said — You're an old hand at this, aren't you? — and he winked and shrugged as the mike began again to catch the milling throng — The thought at once occurred to me, it did, that if all of us in this country were to unite like one man and raise hands, it would be a great cause, well, I don't know, but a great cause, if all thirty-six million of us linked up and showed how many of us there really are...

— Pushing thirty-seven million now... — someone interjected from the side. — The latest statistics...

— Well thirty-seven then; it'll be a great cause!

— Attention! — shouted the little man in the cyclist's cap — Attention! We're starting now! We're joining hands from the mountains to the sea! Up and down the country, far and wide! I am with you!

People began to retreat in unaccountable panic, but it was too late, for hands had already clenched in tight grips, and the assistants of the man who was directing every movement over the loudspeaker stepped out into the crowd and steered people into line, and in their outstretched arms they caught giggly women trying to abscond, and the chain grew longer and it emerged from the ashen shadow of the palace and bisected the vast square; the pair of them walked slowly backwards unfurling the cloth, checked the slogan, shrugged their shoulders: *Don't Wait to Be Asked Again, Come and Join Our Pure Heart Chain*; and on the side the cameraman froze in a catatonic pose as he recorded an interview; words impressed the passive tape — Our chain alas lacks many, and here I'd like to take the opportunity; the lack of links, but I tell you it can all be put right; a man who no longer feels he's one of us, proof of expiation, admit to errors; one could admit to having erred and overshot the mark, but that's the only road, expiation, it has already, as it were, has been recognized, so to speak, and so to, truth, an attempt, this resentment, this feeling, and now they've exploited, renounced citizenship; it's complex; they left on impulse, it's not easy to tackle; on the one hand they were refused, we know instances of, and so forth, they came back and confessed, not just a question of valid passports; what reasons, what excuses; if he still wants a passport come and say, come and explain and appeal, always appeal — and the chain was growing, snaking already round the corner of the store.

Eager reporters followed the line of people and prodded them with their mikes; the raindrops lashed them even as they averted their faces, but no one had the guts to desert the chain; the wardens circulated through the streets and rounded up passers-by; where, where, which way, join the chain, they urged the recalcitrant; the chain bulged and was now skirting the bank; with an automatic pistol slung over his shoulder, a guard stood like a post on the stone steps, muttering monotonously in his beard — Dollars, dollars, anyone got any hard currency to sell? — the chain grabbed and swallowed him before he had time to realize he was already one of the links; on one side a sinewy woman gripped him in her chapped palm, on the other a boy with a topknot died willow-green; the guard bridled and tugged away in a bid to reach for his pistol, but he was in no state to make such a move.

— And what does the chain mean to you? — the reporter cried. — What do these pure hearts mean to you? — he jabbed the man standing nearest with his mike. Like one roused from a trance, he shook himself and answered in a quiet voice — Basically I'm for porn. Specially when several knock up one woman, get me? Though I don't fancy women with dogs...

And his neighbour, while squeezing his hand in her whitened fingers, protested violently; her cheeks went puce and she choked, then controlled her coughing — Oh no, dearie, society's not up to it. It's nauseating. Not even stimulating. In the lower orders it's popular for one woman and two...

— Why not? — the man said in a suppressed voice. — When that's what she wants? In that case lay her, that's what I say — and he was seized by a paroxysm of thinnish laughter, but the reporter had long since moved on.

The chain now ran along the alleys, then straightened out in a wide avenue; the little man in the cyclist's cap stood in the open car with his mike, roaring over the loudspeaker to the chain, turning dangerously purple — News has reached us that the chain from the southeast is getting ever closer; let us unite midway and when we unite let's raise our hands aloft for joy; let's give it a trial run: hands up — he bellowed over the loudspeaker. The chain tensed but its hands compliantly ascended and froze in the air. Soon it began to droop, for it was laden with nets and bright bags from foreign supermarkets. An emaciated blond youth in a jacket with an upturned collar alone had his hands free; gripping his leather bag between his teeth for convenience, he leaned forward from the rank; his tongue lisped against the artificial leather — My pure heart bearth gifth for the Party — and he craned his neck perilously forward, but no microphone succeeded in capturing his voice. — That boss — someone said grudgingly as the car and loudspeaker moved away — that chain boss, he knows what makes a duck quack all right; for every bod he rounds up. he gets ten groszy cash in hand. So do your sums, mister — and he jerked his head violently as though to resist suffocation — for ten he gets one zlot, right? Ten zlots for a hundred. A hundred for a thousand. A thousand for ten thousand. And Bob's your uncle, enuf for half a litre. No work involved.

— He'll get a medal for the chain. And a bonus for the medal — someone chipped in.

— You bet. 'specially as it's all anti-subversion — the man jerked his head — Must be a medal. For a start there's the half-litre. When he rounds up twenty thousand, there's two half-litres. Enuf! He won't round up thirty thousand, but he can have a good binge all the same. Son of a bitch! — the man tossed his head about in a rage till ripples went down the chain.

The head of the chain had moved far away, passing a gate where an old man stood staring at the sky, spitting out words that ricocheted; from the corner of his eye he saw the chain approaching and shouted all the louder as though he hoped to be heard — Lookie folks, I've had sixty-five years' slog and grind from dawn to night and what, bus tickets eighteen a ride; from dawn to night; slog and grind, slog away grey-head, you stupid old grey-head — and he pummeled his forehead with his fists and stamped. The chain grabbed his hands as though to spare his head, took him in noiselessly and careered down the street.

A car drew up alongside the chain and out jumped a cameraman and some other fellow who wanted to latch on. The cameraman focused his lens, but there was an outcry and the man hesitated — Blumin' cheek, you weren't standing here, now were you, confess; and the man jumped back into the car, the cameraman followed suit and off they drove.

The chain wound round a statue; iron figures in tin coats ready to shoot from antiquated rifles huddled on the plinth; all stared through steely eyes in one direction and in that direction the chain expanded and slowly approached the Monopol shop; a woman drenched to the skin stood in front of the shop, and two men held a banner with a flowery inscription above her head: *You Don't Need Alcohol to Have Fun*; another man stood swaying in front of them shouting — Bravo, bravo — he stifled his hiccoughs and laughed, and rain mingled with the tears on his cheeks — Bravo; it's three months since I came off the booze, and I've only got nine months to go before I'm awarded a small coronation sword; only nine more months to go; that sword's the brainchild of the DT colleagues in our anti-alcohol group and they've made it so that two years off the bottle gets you a larger sword, and three years an even larger one; that big, big as a chicken — and he spread out his hands to demonstrate the size of the sword; that's just what the crowd was waiting for, and it scooped him up from outside the Monopol shop; a man leaped out of the doorway squeaking; the squeak issued from under his jacket, and he spoke feverishly, adjusting his collar and looking helplessly round; only a trampled banner with the flowery message separated him from the people in the chain, *You Don't Need Alcohol to Have Fun*; and some rapt journalist was noting the fervent words of a girl in his soggy notebook — For me the chain means everything and from this time on I'm going to be a completely different person, because I have seen that I'm not alone, that we are legion — the man's eyes lit up; he took the journalist gently by the elbow and led him into the doorway; the journalist walked instinctively, paying no heed and jotting down the last words — I love the chain — and the damaged shortwave transmitter gave a soft squeal...

A woman in the chain glanced at her neighbour and squeezed his fingers meaningfully; he stooped towards her and started humming in a flat tenor — No one knows just how wonderful you are — and she passed her tongue over her lips and whispered — You're a cute little nightingale...

— We can always find a way — her neighbour resumed, bowing his head, but at that moment a car came roaring by — Hands up for a trial run; the northeast has crossed over the Vistula — and the cyclist's coloured cap flashed past; the couple's hands rose submissively, and they turned away from each other like strangers.

— Is your sector for or against? — a frozen pedestrian enquired in sudden interest, clapping his wet beret against his knees like a Cossack dancer.

— Depends... — uncertain voices replied.

— What I mean is... For the Party or against?

— It varies...

— Because the sector in the passage there's shouting Lech, Lech, and one fellow's singing '*I've flushed my Socialist Youth badge down the bog*', and round the corner they're crying long live the second stage of the economic reform and *We go along with PRON all the way*. In the square they're singing religious stuff... Well?

— Yes and no...

— Not really...'Cause I don't know...Where'm I to join?

— And you mister...I meantersay...

— You tell first...

— It varies... I've joined the chain because my wife ditched me for another guy. And it hurts.

— I know it hurts — the passer-by replied. — What's more it's meant to...

— You just go up to the front and ask there. They'll tell you. 'Cause we...what've we...We were told to stand here, that's why. Mind you, there might be a flash on the box...a treat for the kids. The TV's passed by once this way but they didn't film us. Next time maybe. How can we know what the chain really...?

— They say it's to build bridges... to be socially-minded...

The far end of the chain distended in zigzags, warily sidestepping the puddles churned up by the wheels of a passing car; a purple face flashed by in the rain, booming from the car roof — My heart is pure, is yours? Southwest getting close! Hands aloft! Joy! Joy!

A lacework of hands poised in mid-air...

Hard by the church a subdued queue was washed down by the rain; women whispered cautiously among themselves

— I'm standing in for my hubby as he couldn't...a perfectly valid excuse...

— Standing in...

— 'Cause my hubby couldn't ... actually he's drunk, but perhaps he'll cure him from a distance, that miracle-healer ...

— Can't do it, not from a distance — the women started whispering. — His powers don't reach that far.

— He must lay his hands in person...

— He doesn't cure drunkenness.

— He cures everything ... Here's my husband's ticket...

— How can he heal him? Where's he to lay his hands? On his throat?

— I suppose so...Where else?

— What sort of an illness is it if a man drinks? It's worse when he don't work. Then he's not a man. Can't call him a man, not if he don't work. He's not a man. I'm not saying he's a child. But he has to drink, 'cause otherwise he won't work...

The chain was getting closer and the women lining up outside the healer's now noticed it and shuffled uneasily and craned forward, shielding their watery eyes with their palms — What is it, what is it? — the women murmured. — What d'ya mean? I guess it's a method of linking hands to create a current and the current passes through and cures everything; they say it's better than laying on of hands when a current like that strikes; what d'ya mean better, laying on of hands is far the best; they say the current's better; I've had the current four times; but why've they come barging along here with that current of theirs; they can go back where they came from; it's obvious why; to have a choice of cure; there's two ways of looking at it; I'm not budging, I've got me ticket for laying on of hands, I'm not going to waste me ticket; then you stay put, no one's forcing you, see; say what you like, a current's a current — and individual silhouettes start to slip away from the line of women and head toward the chain, with hands outstretched...

— North's approaching! North's getting closer every minute! Latest news, the North is at the city gates! — the loudspeaker howled from the car roof, and bloodshot eyes closely assessed the row of people. — Today we'll join the whole country in a chain! Tomorrow we'll unite the entire globe! Now for a trial run! Hands up! — and hands rose and gleamed like bronze in the rain. And the chain turned beyond the receding car and overtook the women at the sacristy door.

— What'll the chain change deep down in your life? What? — the reporter quizzed, prodding her expansive breasts with the mike, while the woman attempted to collect her thoughts; she bit her lips, and her neighbour poked his head from between raised shoulders and whispered in a pained voice — This system has its merits...

The lady reporter charged up and down the ranks — What system, what merits — voices on either side soared above the raised hands — what, which system, what merits, that man asked; now what was it you said about the merits of the system; just what is it you have it mind; what did I say? there we go; but who said, say what you like the system has its merits; I said nothing of the sort; you must've dreamed it madam, sure you're feeling all right? — and the man attempted to lower his hands as though to shield himself, but was unable to move; the chain overhead was so strong that it lifted his feet momentarily off the ground.

And people exchanged uncertain glances, warily poking their heads beyond the pure hearts chain — It won't come off with the menfolk; I ask you, how could it, where's their sense; how, where...

— Without 'em it'll be another mighty flop, I'm telling you; one great awful mighty flop, oh-h-h — the woman trying to answer the reporter's question began to lament.

— Our chain'll get us going! Our chain'll get the country going again! — words from the distant loudspeaker rattled against the massive house walls.

— What's that? What chain? — someone in the line was intrigued.

— Us. We're the chain, the chain is us. You're the chain too.

—What, me?

— Then whataya standing there for?

— We'll know in good time. They'll end up telling us what. Issue some communiqués... I'll give you chain, you scum — and the man lunged at his neighbour, but the chain didn't flinch.

A vanload of militiamen now entered the street and upon sighting the chain of pure hearts, the driver instinctively slowed down; keen eyes glimmered behind the panes but quickly dimmed as the van accelerated; its blue pulsating light flailed the faces of those standing there and a dark streak focused on them just one moment more, then streamed away noiselessly.

Both ends of the chain are growing, even though the wardens are nowhere to be seen and the rain carries darkness above the roofs; the last cameraman and reporter jump into the car and set off; they drive past a wall of people, and the reporter sits comfy in the shadow muttering to himself — It's like drawing a sickle out of an arse, that chain...

The ends of the chain progress at their own pace and prowl between the houses; rare passers-by link on — I'm sort of for this chain, though I can't say how I feel about things — confides a subdued voice, then falls silent...

Suddenly one end of the chain passes beyond the bend in the wall and freezes in its tracks as it comes face to face with the other end, which has come the wrong way, and both ends look at one other, bewildered; they are separated by no more than a narrow strip of lawn, but by now the street is empty and the chain goes limp; each end eyes the other; — They were meant to be across the Vistula long ago; or maybe we were meant to...— and a voice crescendos — Trial run! hands up! hands up! — the open car with the little man in the cyclist's cap emerges from round the bend, and when he sees both ends of the chain, he turns frantically white, stupefied to silence; the car speeds past in a veil of watery dust and mist as the man thumps his fists against the cabin, then whips his cap from his head, chucks it to the ground and runs it over...

As the car vanishes for good in the dark, a hoarse bellowing blares from the loudspeaker on the roof:

— Not that way, ca-a-nt! Not that way!

A Sense of

High up, as far as a man can reach: *KOR = Jews*\! And just
below: *You're a Jew too, you Jew*\!

They were old graffiti, scratched with a sharp implement
on the blackened wall of the elevator; no longer erasable.

The man shifted as he stared in amazement at the letters
and moved his fingers along the groove, then succumbed,
pulled out a pen and pressed with his thumb; but the spring
shot up like a spark; shadows suddenly flapped desperately
overhead and he felt a knock in the air, and panic; raising
his head, he saw a scared pigeon battling beneath the ceiling till finally it clung to the metal contraption that made
it impossible to steal the light bulb, and the shadows of its
wings froze; the man gasped for air and, when he recovered,
extracted a bottle from under his trouser belt, flicked off the
stopper, raised it to his mouth and drank, looking sideways
at the pigeon that hung bat-like beneath the bulb.

The man slowly aimed his finger at the button and
pressed it without withdrawing his hand; the elevator set
off in violent downward jolts; again he raised the bottle, but
missed the mark and vodka spilled over his chest.

So he drew his stomach in deep and began to tuck the
stopper-less bottle behind his belt when some slips of paper

and photographs fluttered down his loose trouser leg and splayed at his feet like a pack of cards; some of the photos were turned picture side up; others, shiny white, were scrawled over with notes; at his feet lay the picture of a factory in a forest, barricaded by an open-work concrete fence, the other side of which pipes sprawled and bulged at one end like tank barrels, a railway siding with a row of trucks and blurred human figures holding flashlights in the dark, solemn people grouped round a priest at a table; the man moved his leg and unwittingly trod on a small snapshot of two withered women standing in the snow above a black stain that looked like the remains of dried blood; with a whine the elevator plummeted down the shaft.

Silence and mist covered the vast square; its houses lay in decay, unreal as a stage backcloth: jutting balconies stacked with discarded objects, broken chairs, faded children's toys, scraps of refuse, dusty jars and bottles, saucepans with holes and cracked enamel, voiceless TV boxes, old-fashioned chandeliers, rotting picture frames, rusty bikes, strung-up bundles of old newspapers.

The wind occasionally whipped up the mist, driving along plastic yoghurt containers that rattled like Purim ratchets...

A weathered scrap of cardboard hung in the window of a closed-down kiosk with the words, Special Offer: Buy a calendar with your dreambook and receive a free gift poster for the 300th anniversary of the Relief of Vienna.

These houses were alien here, built provisionally, as though the old proprietors of other apartments in no longer

existing houses would soon return and bring the neighbourhood to life.

Several leafless trees stood still in the square, and the pile
of black snow turned to bone beneath them, like charnel ice.

The sparse weeds failed to cover the trampled earth,
from which rusty jar-tops and fragments of glass protruded;
again the mists turned about bearing heavy scraps of newspaper and stifled guttural cries and the shrill of a whistle.

The man stood swaying outside the building, looking,
faltering, pressing his eyelids: — It's so dark, is there an
eclipse today? Maybe the eclipse's today, the ecl...

— Mister. What eclipse? — he heard a voice and removed his fingers from his swollen eyelids and blinked, but
no image emerged out of the mist opaque as a bladder.

— That's no eclipse. There was a better one yesterday.
It's just a rum sort of mist today. It sticks to you. Stifles you.
Like it always does.

— For a split second I couldn't see — the man said. — I
thought there might be an eclipse today...

— Not today there's no eclipse. It's Women's Day today.
There was even a pep-talk on the radio this morning telling
us to love our womenfolk today. They have their feast day
too. It's not an eclipse. It's the wrong date. But there was a
better one yesterday. Or the day before. Nothing doing. I'm
here. And you're facing the other way.

And the man spun round, strained his bloodshot eyes
and saw an old man standing there.

— So that's where you are — he said. — Because I was beginning to think I was talking to myself. And where's Gensia?

— What Gensia?

— Gensia Street. Where is Gensia Street? I can't seem to find it.

— What Gensia? There's no such street. You've come on a wild goose chase...

— What do you mean, no such street? It's here on the map.

— It may've been once. But how long ago? Anyway it's all gone. Anielewicz* is where Gensia used to be. I remember Gensia. Doesn't exist now. It's gone.

— So where's Gensiowka?

— What Gensiowka...

— The prison in Gensia Street. Gensiowka. I'm looking for Gensiowka. I know someone there. Political. In Gensiowka. It must be documented.

— There's no Gensiowka. It's gone. Way back in Gomulka's day. How can you know someone there if it doesn't exist? It's gone. I just remember the demolition and how those idiots made a beeline for the walls. With pickaxes. Spades. You name it. Crowbars. Grubbing for the gold left by the Jews. Greedy for what the Jews had left. And where

* Street named after the leader of the Warsaw Ghetto Uprising.

of all places? In prison. Thought it was walled up. Ignorant, deluded lot. They saw Jewish gold everywhere. In prison walls. You name it. Chisels. Exhaust pipes. Bare nails. There's stupidity for you, eh? Like Mongols. Like locusts. You've got into a right twist with that Gensiowka of yours, 'cause I know every inch of this place. I'm applying for the keeper's job.

— I went up in the elevator — the man said — to see the view from the top floor. 'Cause I can't find it. But there're no windows on the stairway. So I came down again and I'm still looking. Melted into thin air, that Gensiowka. Someone I know's inside.

— It's gone, mister. Everything here's gone. This is the ghetto. All that remains of Gensiowka is this naked square. Here. See? Here. Where we're standing. There was a pit where this knoll is now. A dark cell. A pit. Here. I know every inch. This square. You can't see it now because of the mist. Know what I mean?

— Then perhaps he's not inside. Only playing. That rings a bell. I could've got it wrong. If he's not inside he might be playing. Playing in Gensiowka. That should be documented too.

— It's all the ghetto here. Sometimes the ground spits up a brick. Like from a cellar. Those bricks come crawling out of the earth.

— Yeah, I got it muddled. He plays here. The politicals play football here once a week. The prisoners. I got it wrong. Because either he's inside, or he's playing. So first I thought he was inside. Now I remember in fact he's playing. Not inside.

— Some rascals were kicking a ball around here. Old men. And they're still at it. Politicals, you say? What d'ya mean? There's only bones and ashes under the turf. I thought they must be hooligans. Strange that someone wants them to be playing football here. Acting on orders, like. But for politicals to play football? In a cemetery? Mind you, it used to be Jewish. So it's nobody's. So everybody makes a grab. Are you sure?

— They play here. Once a week. I keep records.

— I even thought of chasing them off — the old man said. — Only I was afraid they'd sack me on the spot. But I will in due course. When I take over as keeper. 'Cause at present I got no right to interfere. This area's called Amusement Park Square. There's an information board. Regulations. Not to throw litter. No cycling. There's something about ponds in the regulations, but it's been painted over. Where's there a pond here? Not to litter the ponds. There's never been a pond here. So they painted over the ponds. All under the heading Amusement Park Square. Politicals you say? And where we're standing there was a sewer manhole during the Jewish uprising. Here. A manhole. They were political too. Yes or no? It looks to me that as a nation we've had it for good and all. And stinking crazy beyond hope. I mean. From every point of... Not long ago some folks drove up here in a Polonez**. I know everything. They jumped out and started throwing things at the memorial. See the streamers hanging there. No one cleans up. It was eggs, only you can't see it in this mist. The old woman just barely dragging her feet, leaning on that boy. His neck is bruised. Father carrying the child. His hands are bruised. And that's the way they go to Stawki, to the train. That's where they loaded them, where the filling station is. What's the politics behind it all. To come bumbling along with a filling station in Deportation Square? That's politics for you. But to come bumbling along and play football on the ruins? Just as well the mist hides it all. When I get the job, I'll chase 'em all off, I will. Only how to get the job? 'Cause the secretary took offence and put me down as blind on my identity card. What do they mean, blind? I'm trying for the keeper's job, but they keep saying how can I be a keeper when I'm blind. So I tell 'em and show 'em I can see. They say that on my identity card I'm blind. Blind, me? They tell me to change my card. But how can I change my card when I'm already registered as blind. That blindness is going to stick to me, they'll stamp it in my next card too. And I can see everything. Over there on the other side there's a glass case. Youth festival. And there's photos. A tug-o'-war. Some have completely curled up at the edges. The tug-o'-war's still OK. You can't see it from here, but I know. You won't be able to see, but I can.

**Communist-era motor vehicle produced in Poland 1978-2002.

Dusty photos. In the middle of the square there's a sandpit for kiddiwinks. Faced with old bricks. From the ghetto. That's also politics for you. If I got that keeper's job, I could clear up a few things around here. Though mind you, I'm scared. Might get the sack. That there was the tram route before the war. Okolna line.

— It will all have to be documented — the man muttered as he thoughtlessly touched his stomach; he came sharply to his senses, grabbed his trousers in his fist and began to fumble and to shove his palms under his belt... He stiffened and whispered — My documents have been stolen...disappeared. Photos. Notes. Everything. All that travelling. Train journeys. Where haven't I been! Just came back from a place where they built blocks in the 'fifties in the shape of Stalin's name. But you could only see it from the air. It was only later, when they built annexes, that the word vanished. I had it all in a file. I found a factory in a forest and I'm sure it's for armaments, 'cause why else would it be in a forest; I had a photo...

The photo left behind in the elevator showed a factory in a forest, circled by a concrete fence, and with sprawling pipes; patches of melting snow turned dark, revealing a garbage-heap of medicine packings left over from the autumn railway robbery; a siren sounded for break, the broadcasting system started up, and jaunty music swamped the square; when it broke off, voices of the staff could be heard, recorded at the end of a long-forgotten year, but the announcer had no other recordings — How has this last year been? Was there anything special? If it's names you're after,

I'm not mentioning anyone; no, no, it's not names we want, just was there anything special; special? no; then perhaps something different; nothing different; then maybe some important day; important, the only important day will be the first day in the New Year, I mean tomorrow. — Workers' protest basically justified — another voice spoke up — basically a small group exploited class dissatisfaction; yes, yes, but was there anything different about the year that's ending; different? no; then maybe something special; special, well, we had that vote in the trade union; but was anything different for you; not one iota; work is basically stultifying, just running round the old treadmill; and what would you wish for, madam, in this year coming hard on us; nothing for me personally, but I can't speak for others. — Then the courtyard was flooded with lively music, which startled a flock of birds that fluttered over the gate inscribed with the words in English, *Long live Peace...*

The watery mist above the square revealed the rubble of the building. The grey windows on the first floor were plastered over with crisscross strips of paper. Next to the dry cleaners, workmen had abandoned their excavation half-finished; soil remained heaped above the trench along with swollen crumbs of amber bricks and the shreds of disused milk canisters that had once secreted important papers.

A cry rent the cloak of mist — *Goal, goal* — then shouting, and a dull whistle.

— Did you hear that? — the old man said. — Scoring goals. Confound 'em. It's in the regulations in black and white that visitors to the park and the greens are forbidden to use cycles or other vehicles, to destroy the architecture or park facilities, or dig pits. Now they're playing football. Scoring goals. There's no paragraph in the regulations for that. Not even under common sense.

But the man was not listening, he was patting his stomach just to make sure. — See, friend, I didn't even notice them steal the stuff; all my work lost in a jiff; I had everything on file: photos; people on a loading platform; train carriages; checking what goes to the East in those wagons, at night; quite a dab hand at photography...

And the flashlights on the platform blinked; numerous figures stooped in the dark; people with cold-stiff fingers dug out from the snow lumps of coal dropped from the trucks while unloading during the day; bags and briefcases bulged, hands weighed every stone and clump of snow — Go on, scoop up all you can, man; how much can you dig away like that — a figure straightens up, and the light is switched off to spare the batteries. — When I was picking up coal once during the German occupation, the railway sentry fired a shot at me and missed, which is why I'm still at it now; otherwise I'd have long since bitten the dust — and the light flashed again, and fingers begin to sift the snow...

— Yes, yes. Folks used to roll up when that lot was playing, wanting to join in — the old man said. — But it was no go. They had their own teams and wouldn't let 'em join in. And they always played with a sort of a frenzy, kicking so hard, yessir, that their legs groaned.

And the owner of a car stepped slowly backwards on the lawn and cocked his head to examine the car, then lunged forward, pulled out a rag and rubbed away some stains with a blob of foam, and shifted backwards again with his head to one side. — There's a guy here that's always washing his car; I'd chase him away for that, yessir, but I'm too scared; might get sacked...Washing his car...

The man stooped to insert his hand knee-high up his trouser-leg, then straightened up with a resigned air.

— And the cozy chat with the priest? What? — he cried, striking his forehead with the palm of his hand.

The room in the photograph was squalid, scantly furnished, the rickety table covered in oil-cloth; a priest sat at the table, a surpliced acolyte crouched behind his back, and a family stood solemnly around him; the father of the family lay on a pallet at the back of the room, propped on his elbow.

And he broke into a hoarse cough, then tried to raise himself and sit up, but immediately fell back on his elbow; all he could do was shout through his coughing and wag his finger at the people by the table.

— The missis drinks! The daughter drinks! Son-in-law drinks! Grand-daughter drinks! I'm the only one in the family that doesn't drink! They all drink!

— And who was it went to a brothel in Warsaw? Even before the war? — the old woman bellowed from the table. —Who?

— But I paid! — the old boy wheezed.

— If you paid, it's in order — the priest laughed to himself and scooped an envelope up from the table.

— I pay for my own booze — the son-in-law shouted arrogantly.

— If it's your money, it's no sin — the priest mumbled, then rose and made for the door, pushing the absent-minded acolyte before him. No sooner in the hall he opened the envelope, had a quick look and handed it to the acolyte — Enter it on the chart, but do get it right; always check, one always must check in case they've stuffed newspaper in the envelope...

The stamping of feet could be heard through the thick mist, and the hoarse breathing of the football players, and cries of pain.

— Fancy a drop? — the man asked.

— I don't drink — the old man said as he ran his hand over the brown stones facing the sewer manhole — 'Cause I can't. If I could, I wouldn't say no. — And he bent over the inscription, mouthing the words.

— All fuckin' useless — he said. — But if they'd survived, they'd have had another twenty-five years to go to the anniversary. And another deportation. From the Gdansk station to Vienna. It's not far. Just beyond Deportation Square. It all came to an end in one spot. Like it was a question of politics. Or mere convenience. But nowadays? Where's the convenience? What's the politics? Why keep tormenting them? Torment the living. Torment the dead. They even torment the memorial. A pile of bricks. What sort of politics is that? Where's the sense? All fuckin' useless. Fuckin' useless. There's nobody, not even to weep.

But the man was not listening, only staring at the round manhole and frowning — To have lost that file, he brooded, — All those documents... The manhole opens and out they come, for they were there.

— What? — asked the old man.

— No. Nothing. It's lost for good. It can't be compiled again. All filed away you know where. I had a photo of a woman at the spot of the tragedy. Blood on the snow. It was in someone's interest for it not to see the light of day.

The photo he had trampled in the elevator showed the shadowy silhouettes of two women standing in the snow; between them a black stain like dried blood; the express flew past — It must be six, around six or seven; must be between six and seven; it flew past just a second ago.

— The way we work, no clock, no time — the woman said.

— So the two of them drank and drank with nothing to eat, then one fell asleep, so for a bite the other cut out a piece of his buttock with his penknife, what a surprise when he wakes up and finds a snack, and he bled away and they found him stiff, just here, he was dead in no time; the two of them were drinking in the bushes here, and the blood vanished completely.

— Maybe he froze? 'Cause there's not much blood.

— Maybe, maybe he did. But with a penknife they said, for a snack. As a surprise. Where's the sense?

The old man was listening to the sound of the football match; he cupped his hand to his ear and raised his head high like a blind man.

— All that trouble for nothing. And who'll believe it all now? — the man said, he pulled in his stomach, reached inside his trouser belt for the bottle. He thrust back his head, as though listening to the match like the old man, then took a swig and spoke bitterly — To get the hell out of here at last, emigrate as far away as possible; enough of this struggle, how much can a man take; I'd like to be a bootblack in New York, in a street with theatres, and shine the shoes of actors and producers and spend all my dough on going to the theatre and see more and more plays and get to know the different actors and shine their shoes and whisper something to each of them: try entering the stage from a different angle, keep that frown for later, more expression there, and in time it will be clear that my every remark has its impact, that he's polishing and perfecting his style, and over the years I become the best shoeshine man in New York, and the actors and producers flock to me, for everything I say turns out to be true, all the theatres need me, their success depends on me and I pull all the strings, and that's when I choose to die and everyone sees what a void I've left and they can't do a thing without me and they look for me and all those celebrity actors and producers come at last to the shabby little room where I lived and in that shabby little room they find everything I was most attached to all those years and all they see is my copy of *Pan Tadeusz* and a handful of native soil...*** What's left for me to do here? You simply can't make a move. I've already done my bit. The

*** Poland's national epic, by Adam Mickiewicz, 1834.

young can get on with it now. It's their turn.

— Yeah, yeah — the old man said. — And when they had the bright idea of building a filling station in Deportation Square, they forgot to make underground tanks. So the first petrol went straight into the earth. Thousands of litres. That's their policy for you: National Petroleum — Umschlagplatz. ****

— I'm not going to stick my neck out any longer — the man said, pulling in his belly and reaching beneath his belt.

— That thirty-storey block you can see from everywhere, they've been building it for the last twenty-five years and they can't get it finished — the old man said. Because they built it on the site of a synagogue. And the rabbi cursed it. He did, I tell you.

— When I still had a wife, my wife always used to say it's like fighting windmills — the man reflected. — That no one will appreciate the effort. And now? Now that I'm empty-handed?

The wind parted the mist. The players had finished their game and stood apart, bending down as though looking for something, heavily gasping for air.

— Seem to have stopped playing — the old man strained to listen. — At one time they didn't even want to play, refused in fact, 'cause the whole pitch was mucked up and the local riffraff brought their dogs onto the pitch; how can you play in a cesspit? That was when someone lit a fire under the memorial plaque on Anielewicz' bunker. The bunker's just there; in winter, mothers take their children tobogganing there and the kids come sailing down from the bunker;

the heat from the fire cracked the stone... They didn't fancy playing then, oh no...

— Can't you chase them away?

— Beg your pardon?

— Couldn't you get a stick? And chase them away? Give them a thrashing?

— Wouldn't mind chasing 'em. But I haven't got permission. And no way to get it, 'cause the secretary took offence and put me down as blind...

— Forget about permission. Next time they play you could give them a sound walloping, those politicals, and I'd take photographs. I'll bring a camera; you lick 'em, I'll snap 'em. And then you slash their ball with a knife. That'll be a document for you. Well? — the man got enthusiastic and leaned forward and focused his eyes on the mist that separated him from the players till he could no longer see them.

The old man had stopped listening; he turned away and moved off with upraised head as though wanting to hear the road before him; he stepped softly, placing his footsteps with care, and was concealed by the wing of the dark memorial, and by the mist.

— Well? Fancy a drop? — the man brightened up. And how about those Jews? What? As you were saying. Fancy a drop?

**** The railway sidings in Warsaw from which Jews were herded off to Treblinka and other Nazi concentration camps.

And he peered about on all sides, then pressed his fingertips on his swollen eyelids and mumbled — An eclipse, it's an eclipse, everything's dark, it's an...

World of Worlds

A monotonous dawn settles on the town and darkness slowly seeps back into the porous walls.

Outside the food store two tramps slept heavily on a broken park bench; sleep had dazed them the previous evening, before the shop closed, before they had emptied their beer bottles; since then they'd been clutching those bottles between stiffened hands, not spilling a drop; the light silvered their stubble.

White fluff drifted from the slender poplars and shrouded their heads, shoulders, thighs and knees, so that they looked like two down-at-heel angels; one of the angels shuffled his swollen feet along the paving stone; probably dreaming he was on the run...

A truck drew up alongside the curb, its motor died, and the driver's head collapsed onto the steering wheel; the glassy horn stirred the birds in the crowns of the poplars, but the sleepers on the park bench didn't budge.

A dour delivery man lowered the back hatch and pulled out crates of bottles that tinkled like Japanese bells and swung them into a pyramid, one on top of the other; when the tip of the pyramid began to lurch, he hitched a steel poker to the bottom crate, leaned forward like a barge-hauler and struggled towards the glass door of the shop, till his flushed brow touched the pane; he rested quietly, then roused himself and returned to the van and heaved more crates, crashing them against the concrete as though to stifle his own pain.

— What an unholy racket those crates make — an unexpected voice came out of the darkness that still prevailed along the wall of the neighbouring house.

— What's the point of delivering so much soda water? When there's no food to be had, for love or... All that bloomin' soda stuff...

— We'll end up eating it.

—Or worse.

The man dragged his pyramid of crates toward the shop, pressed his forehead against the cool glass; just then a large insect scuttled out through a crack in the doorway, paused by the crates and twitched its long feelers.

— A cockroach, a cockroach — voices exclaimed.

— Kill it! Kill the cockroach!

— That's no cockroach. That's a grasshopper.

— Grasshopper my foot. That size? And black? It's a cockroach!

— It's not a cockroach! I knows a cockroach when I sees one. It's a grasshopper I tell you.

— Look at the size of it! A grasshopper'd be greenish-like.

— And it 'ud hop — someone chipped in. — And this 'ere beastie don't hop. It just scuttles.

— Maybe it's had too much to eat...

— Too much to eat! When all they've delivered is soda water. Eaten too much soda water!

— Well then, drunk on soda water.

— You're drunk on soda wateryerself, mister. That'll sure be a cockroach.

And the man withdrew his heated brow from the pane and without a word lifted the metal bar with which he'd been hauling the crate above his head, froze for a moment in that splendid gesture, then struck the insect with such gusto that sparks flew from the paving stone.

— Wow. Did 'im in with a poker. That cockroach I mean — a woman's voice piped up.

— Grasshopper. He'd have been scared to bash a cockroach.

— He missed anyway.

— Maybe he wanted to miss. He didn't have to, not unless he wanted to.

Two men were heading in the direction of these dull voices; they stopped to shake hands, then looked about — You going to the passport bureau too? — one of them asked. — Yeah, sure — and again they peered round — It can't be far from here — the darkness that concealed the building was slowly falling awayto reveal a long line of people clinging to the ashen wall.

— Are you last? — one of the men asked.

— I don't know — the woman replied. I've got number hundred and twelve and I'm hanging on to it. At the front there's a social committee with a list. You have to sign on.

— A hundred and twelve — this early?

— Why, we've been here since one a.m. I've only just come along, so I'm a hundred and twelve.

— Names, please! — startled by a voice from behind, they turned about, but it was only the committee chairman gripping a slim notebook tightly between his fingers, so they gave their names, and he wrote them in angular, technical calligraphy in the appropriate column and said — You're a hundred and thirteen and a hundred and fourteen; we check the list through every hour; anyone not here drops out; I'm going up to the front.

— A hundred and fourteen. That means standing here all day — said the man.

— No, not quite, at the latest till midday — a hundred and twelve replied, then fell silent.

— We'd better stick it out — the man said. — Because right now they appear to be granting passports. Maybe we could take it in turns.

— Oh, no — the woman interjected. — The number has to be confirmed personally. Otherwise, you're dropped from the list. Rules is rules.

They did not reply.

— The office doesn't open till eight — the woman volunteered. — A good couple of hours to go.

One of the men pulled out a packet of cigarettes.

— Beats our last meeting, eh?

— Yeah, how 'bout that mechanic who came along and poked about in the wires behind our bench, because they thought the bugging system had broken down? We were just keeping quiet...

— And that taxi driver looking for his passenger who'd just dropped in, but didn't come out again. He kept asking if there was any other exit, but the duty sergeant denied it. I was summoned again twice, and I got to know that taxi driver. He kept popping in to enquire after his passenger and reckoning how much he'd clocked up on the meter to date. Till they were sick and tired of him. Six months later they admitted his passenger'd been amnestied. The taxi driver emigrated and returned to his profession. Now he's lecturing in mathematics at some university abroad.

— That bugging was a good scene for a story. Did you write anything?

—No.

— Nor did I.

— Quite honestly I didn't know how. It's like that with everything now. I don't know what to write about. What's important. What will be important in the future. They're envious in the West that we have such an interesting country to write about. But I don't know what's so interesting about it. Or what's essential. It's misted over. Washed away. Like soap suds. And that is the essence of our times, of our epoch in general: grey froth. And everyone's writing memoirs now. Diaries. Publishing their notebooks. Everybody's escaping into the past. Publishing underground. Overground. A deluge of notebooks. Everyone's escaping into the past. No one is capable of taking on the present.

— On the one hand there's an indefinable, elusive greyness. On the other, myths. How does one fight a myth? Fight mythology? This country wallows neck-deep in it. Always

has done. How does one tackle that? It was always prema-
ture to tackle it. One always had to wait for the myth to
fade. Only it never did. Even stupidity can be sacrosanct in
this country, the sacred cow of the cliché. One day maybe.
Now it would mean sticking one's neck out. Everyone's
bunking off into the past. So am I. Into my own private past.
It's interesting. Meanwhile I'll try to get this passport, rel-
ishing the thought that I can either stay abroad or return to
this country. Or else announce I'm staying and watch how
many people who've already made that decision suddenly
get the wind up. One more snout at the trough.

A young man sneaks up to the line outside the passport
office, hugs the wall and hides his face in his shirt collar,
observing the situation closely...

— Do you think there's any point? — he asks after a moment's acclimatization.

— Point in what?

— In my applying. Will they let me?

— Course they will. They're easy on passports now.

— But I'm fresh from military service.

— That I don't know. In that case you may have to wait
a bit. I don't know.

— Mind you, I haven't done full service. Only a month.
They had to discharge me, seeing I was getting schizo. All
because I couldn't take the weight of military secrets. The
responsibility. I didn't finish the course, handed in my gun.
Is there any point?

— Point in what? — someone else got interested.

— In my applying. Have I got a chance?

— You're bound to. They're pretty easy now.

— But I'm fresh from the army. Though I handed in my gun.

— Now an acquaintance of mine, when his son was born, registered him as a daughter, so she, I mean he, wouldn't be called up. But truth will out: somebody squealed, and he didn't get a passport. The father I mean. As for the daughter, I mean the son, I can't say. There was quite a rumpus. Turned really nasty. In other words, with the military you can never tell. Sometimes they give, sometimes they don't. Just to keep you on the hop.

— Well, I'll be making tracks. If that's how things stand. And he pushed off, hugging the wall as though in search of a prop, then slipped round the corner of the house, casting one last backward glance.

— Well, but what's going to happen to this country? — one of them began to brood. — What next? Will anything more happen to this country?

— For sure. There'll always be something interesting here. Not in our lifetime though. One day, yes. For the time being they'll sink us, they will. And we'll sink ourselves, until we're dead stuck. The rest of the world can do quite nicely without us. Only no one's prepared to believe that we're simply a nuisance. They just refuse to believe it. Things will start happening here again one day. One day. Luckily we won't be around by then. Everyone's fed up to the teeth with us. Left and right. And below. This country bounces about all over the map. Sometimes it's on the map, sometimes it's not. It vanishes in one place, then reappears in another. Round and round in circles. They're sick of us, and afraid. Or rather… apprehensive.

The inert hand of the man asleep on the bench twitched and the bottle instinctively crept up to his mouth; lips thrust forward, imbibed the poplar fluff that had settled in a ring of foam on the bottle-neck; the sleeper choked, but slightly shifted his position, caught his breath, and started yelping while asleep…

A woman dashed up to the line trying to control her panting — Folks — she said looking ahead — folks, do let me skip in here, eh?

— Whatever next. Barger! — and people laughingly shrugged their shoulders without even turning around. The committee chairman, convulsively clutching his slim note-book, emerged at the woman's side.

— Pull the other, it's got bells on — he said, tapping a lean finger on the green cover.

— But I'm an exception, I've been trying to get here for a week, because when they entered my number, the one that's coded in my passport, they got it wrong and keyed me in as a priest. Now they won't let me out of the country, so I'm stuck. You're down as a priest, they say, and a fine sort of priest you are, they say. You work that one out, then we can talk, they say.

— Priest or no priest — the committee chairman replied — That's no concern of mine. But this — he waved the school pad — is what we must abide by — and numerous heads nodded their approval.

— I'm fed up with interesting events by now — one of them said. — I just don't want to be part of it any more. I can't anyway, because I don't know how to write about these interesting events. And that's the only way I could participate. For years I could always find the key; it existed, it was ready. Now one has to write straight, and I can't write straight, because I'm made differently. My brain's Aesopic. And I can't shake off that language of allusion and the old forms, passé though they may be. I'm out of touch with my time. I don't speak the new language. Everything I try to do is impeccable, of course, only unfortunately it's dead. Propaganda. So I go round in circles locked up inside my own world, just like everybody else, and that's my space, just like everybody else. And so we go round in circles. No one wants to stick his neck out. We lack the tools. Make do with substitute forms. Play at waiting.

— Everyone's waiting for something — someone chipped in from the side; in an attempt to catch their words, he stooped forward with his head askew. — Everyone's waiting for something. Only we don't know what for — he said with a blissful smile.

The line stood waiting in drowsy silence. Nothing could move it now; only one woman was watching; she nodded her head and said to no one in particular, without soliciting support — Now my son, the rector in person hands him his coffee, yes; he's got a university diploma, an M.A.— she shook her head in astonishment and fell silent.

— So it's definitely handkerchiefs. Pocket handkerchiefs.

— Hankies, of course. An absolute must.

— And Chinese scarves. With fringe. Brilliant.

— Bed linen. Absolutely essential.

— But where to buy all those hankies? And Chinese scarves with fringe? And linen? Where are we s'posed to buy it all?

— There's just been a bulk delivery to our newsstand. It's so cluttered with bed linen there's no room for newspapers. It's quite handy too, 'cause it's open till ten. We can get it from the newsagent. People come and stock up on bed linen right into the night, since it's open till ten. They sneak past with sheets and stuff way after dark, I tell you.

— Crystals, of course. Irons.

— Irons are unobtainable.

— You're right. Must be organised.

— You say one thing, he says irons. Born yesterday, were you? Am I s'posed to teach you what's what? An old codger like you? Really!

— Fox furs, obviously. Fox furs.

— Ah yes, fox. Sure.

— Plastic jackets, pre-wrinkled.

— Lada spare parts. The lot. Anything we can lay our hands on. Every conceivable wheel valve.

— It all sells like hotcakes to the Soviets. Like proverbial hotcakes.

— Mind you, for Greece it's obviously mixers we want. Lots of mixers.

— All sorts of robots, kitchen gadgets too.

— Tools for Greek craftsmen. Every conceivable tool. Vices, bolts, nuts, screws. Whatever we can get.

— Tape recorders, portable TVs, fox furs.

— Lady, but you don't want foxes for the russkies. You've got it muddled.

— I said it was for Greece. Fox furs.

— For the russkies you mainly want electronic watches. Best of all with a bleep. There's not a russki can resist it.

— And Bulgaria. Gold belts, sunglasses, pendants, earrings. The more the better.

— Alarm clocks for Greece. Don't you dare forget alarm clocks for Greece. Lots of pyjamas. Balls.

— What sort of balls? Large? Small? Footballs or what?

— Any balls, big, small, what have you. They're crazy about 'em.

— If you're going to Greece, gas cylinders are the thing. Any amount. And water heaters, because they haven't heard of them, backward lot. Hairdryers.

— But where are we going to buy it all? The shops are empty. Where are we going to buy it all?

— Well, presumably not in the shops.

— You're coming back via Turkey, madam, right? So buy cotton there, right? So you bring the cotton into Poland, right? Then you're sitting pretty, right? And you start organising your next trip. Because you're sitting pretty.

— I'd rather take electronic bleeper watches. I'm in the trade, they make money out of me, so why not. I'd recommend a lady's garter belt. I crammed up to three hundred and twenty pieces on one belt. That's my limit to date. This season I'll be using a bra too. They're mad on those bleeper watches. They'd gladly kill to have one.

— But where to buy all these marvels, eh?

— If you don't know that, lady, there's no point me talking to you.

— Only Greece. Only Greece.

— It would be my first trip abroad since the seventies — one of them said. — I'm terribly afraid of leaving, because I'm afraid of how things here will look from the other side. I don't mean terror, persecution, poverty, and the rest. What I'm most afraid of is that it may all seem sadly grotesque. Now It's all right to view the grotesquerie from over there. But when I return? How will I stand up to it then? Perhaps the whole trip is senseless? Perhaps I'd better stick to what I'm used to?

— You haven't left yet. Steady on. You haven't left yet — the other one replied.

— Looking at it all, I'm reminded of black Zmijewski.
—Who?

It was daylight by now, but the line strung along the wall outside the passport office was unobtrusive. Newcomers first had to get their bearings before walking up and giving their names to the committee chairman, who assigned them a number. They took up their position at the end and waited and watched awhile to become familiar with the group, get acclimatized and feel like a full-fledged member.

The sunlight smote the two angels asleep on the bench; one of them wanted to shield his eyes, made an uneasy, imprudent move and rolled over the gap in the bench bang onto the concrete sidewalk without spilling one drop from his bottle; the shadow from the metal bar bisected his face from forehead to chin giving the angel a pensive expression as he lay on the pavement; his mate asleep on the bench stretched out his hand and in a trance fumbled the bars by his side where his companion had been lying; his hand ceased moving, and he whimpered...

— I once wrote an article — one of them said. — Things were already getting stagnant, no one wanted or even knew how to write any more, and some of the minor clandestine papers were in real trouble finding authors; it was essential to start a polemic with that article, but no one felt willing or able to take issue with it, and in the end I had to write an attack on my own piece...with a few abusives for good measure in a follow-up letter to the editor...

— Viewed from one angle, it's getting to be more and more like the story of Zmijewski. I once even dreamed I was Zmijewski — the other one said.

— Who on earth is black Zmijewski? What happened to him?

— There was some sort of jamboree in Warsaw in 'fifty-five. Remember?

— Sure.

— Its exact name was the World Youth and Student Festival for Peace and Friendship.

— That's it.

— Well, there was this festival and the delegations flew back to their various corners of Poland and the world, and one girl delegate from Bialystok felt a bit off colour, so to speak. And nine months later all became clear, she gave birth to a black child. She was so involved in the festival, you see. The progressive black delegate was no longer to be identified, so the little boy was given his mother's name, Zmijewski, and grew up in Bialystok. He picked up the local dialect and even their singsong accent. Thereafter it was all predictable. He joined Solidarity, became a major activist in time, then martial law came. He may have been interned, I'm not sure. Let's assume he was. He came out, and after a while he emigrated to the States, where he met other blacks and began to fraternize with them, as with his own kind. But when he tried to persuade them Reagan was the best president they could dream of, they cracked him one on the beak; it became a sort of habit, he proselytizing them for Reagan, they beating him up. And that's the story of black Zmijewski...from Bialystok.

— Black Zmijewski — the other one said in a reverie.

A small Fiat had drawn up outside the passport bureau; its windows were plastered with bright-coloured stickers in several foreign languages, but the largest was in Polish: *I'm Castrol, Your Loyal Oil*; an extra wiper was mounted at the rear and a special plastic fin in front so the car held the road at high speed, also a radio aerial on a special spring and a towing hook shaped like a cat's head jutting out from the car's body... a man jumped out and looked round and saw the line; even as he walked toward it, his vitality ebbed and he shrivelled, hunched and became one among the many; a woman scrutinized the garish car, lost herself in thought, then said — If you ask me, things are the way they are because the whole government's festering with Jews...

— That's it — one of them said after a while. — In a church on the Vistula they're selling the *Protocols of the Elders of Zion.* Quite openly.

— In church, in church — the woman overheard them. — And you're one of those, aren't you now, that claims the country's anti-Semitic? There's a lot of talk right now, there is. And you mean you don't know who's behind it all, eh? Whose interest it's in? You don't know? Eh?

— Do stop pestering — he said quietly, and with an effort.

— He's a fine one — the woman bridled. — He's a fine one, isn't he? — And she shrugged her shoulders. — Did you hear that? — She turned to her neighbour.

— We always helped them — the other woman assented.

— Always. Always. It will all come out now, 'cause they've announced they're going to expose history's blank pages. I mean, when my dad saw them being transported to the camps, he felt awfully sorry for them, felt sick even. And he was a colonel. So there.

A clamour of voices rang out from the cross street, and round the corner a bearded elderly man wearing tight short trousers appeared, followed by a well-disciplined line of children in scout uniforms; they swayed in unison bearing aloft streamers, symbols and totems, and sang mechanically,

Though grey it is our colour,
Our uniforms are grey,
We're brave and bold at heart,
And when we swoop upon our foe,
He's taken off his guard.

The man in the short trousers looked round, saw he'd fallen out of step, marked time to catch the rhythm, and pressed forward on the wave of weary voices,

And I grab the wick and bottle,

Pounce and throw it fast;

If they shoot me for my country,

I shall breathe my living last...

The two feathered angels stirred, raised their eyelids on eyes like carnelians as a satiated sort of smile crept across their faces; both started to stand up as though to test their powers and drank in the words of the song; when the last scout had marched past brandishing the standard, both blew the white rings of poplar dust from the bottles and gulped and spat — Yes, yes — one of them mumbled — that's the way it ought to be, you'd better believe it, youth, youth — and they tottered behind the vanishing parade, overtook it and tried to fall into step. One shook his head the better to regain control — See how they go, that's the way to do it — and they clumsily tried to join in the song, like two guardian angels watching the troop...

— Black Zmijewski? — one of them said.

— From Bialystok — the other replied.

— It's long past the hour — cautious voices murmured.

— It ought've opened a long time ago. It's the same everywhere. Anything to fray the nerves. Anything to harass.

— If it was nothing worse than that — someone reflected. — It's all done with a view to putting us at odds. That's what the present policy is all about.

— But something must be done. They ought've started receiving applications half an hour ago...

— Tell the chairman to do something about it. He couldn't wait to be chairman, now let him do something...

— Chairman, chairman — the chairman was getting worked up. — When anything goes wrong it's always the chairman's fault.

He braced himself, raised his hand and tapped so delicately on the metal door that its plate did not respond.

The line froze in expectation, all ears. — Now you see —the chairman said softly — no sound or si...

He leaned helplessly against the door and hooked his elbow on the handle; as the door gave way slowly, the committee chairman at first stiffened, then retreated, as though choosing to mingle with the crowd...

The people stood still, but since no one appeared in the doorway, heads craned forward; the line began to pulsate gently — What's up, what's going on there, why's no one going in? — Those at the rear lost patience and pressed nearer the door; finally the chairman mustered up his courage, cleared his throat, straightened his shoulders, and led his troop to the back of the waiting room shielding himself with the sixteen-page school pad.

The line crammed its way chaotically in behind him until the surge halted and no one else could squeeze into the room; people inside no longer kept in sequence and those at the back again lost patience and pushed or marked time...

Those who had entered now stood silently hanging their heads, and the committee chairman turned to stone before them... They saw a steep corridor ahead clad in grey oil-painted panelling, and another alien line stretched as far as a grey door with a bulletin board, and was pressing and pushing down that corridor, at the head of which stood another alien committee chairman clutching a slim school pad and entering something on a chart...

As the metal door shuddered halfway open, a woman's torso appeared; she bowed her retreat, paused and bowed again, holding on to the handle, then took another step backwards and was about to close the door, but she stuck her head once more through the narrow crack as though to give one last and final bow, but at the same time pulled the heavy door with all her might and...

Stanisław Barańczak:
Anderman in Context

One of the stories in the present collection by Janusz Anderman encapsulates a symptomatic episode. During an aimless stroll, two young writers discuss literature, or rather, attempt to have a discussion. They have difficulty in formulating any viewpoint. The reason is twofold. The incident takes place in the days of martial law, when, following the unexpected turn of political events and the unprecedented situation in which Polish society then found itself, even to think about writing seemed devoid of any sense. As one of the young men complains, "Everything that has been so far is now a thing of the past." The two are also hamstrung by the presence of their "guardian angel", a secret policeman who shadows their every step and eavesdrops on their every word.

There is nothing in this scene that transcends the canon of realistic description, yet at the same time it is vested with a symbolic dimension. It may be seen as a stark image or metaphor epitomizing the quintessential features of the situation in which Polish literature found itself after December 1981, when the dictatorship of party, policy and army declared war on the nation. Viewed from one angle, the situation was new and unexpected, and it imposed on literature the fundamental and formidable task of interpreting and perpetuating in words the experiences that had altered the collective awareness of society no less than the conceptual world of each individual member of that society. On the other hand, as is often the case in totalitarian states, literature — being by the very nature of things suspected of nonconformity — stood before an elemental danger: it no longer had to fight for freedom of expression alone, but for its very survival.

After December 1981, new forms of police control over culture supplemented the restrictions of censorship that had been in force for decades, ever since the system of prior censorship was introduced at the time of the birth of People's Poland. It was no accident that some of Poland's most interesting writers were to be found among the thousands of internees rounded up in the first days of martial law. It was no mere chance that the Union of Polish Writers, the professional organization that provided help and support for writers, was first suspended, then — in the summer of 1983 — dissolved and replaced by a puppet organization of the same name that was totally subordinated to the authorities and is to this day boycotted by almost all writers of standing. And it was more than just a coincidence that police raids, arrests and draconian court sentences rained with particular relentlessness on those who produce and circulate independent literature: underground publishers, printers and distributors. It is thanks to their combined efforts that, despite persecution and confiscation, several hundred uncensored periodicals and hundreds of uncensored books are still circulating in Poland today.

One of the paradoxes of totalitarian states is that their literature, whilst forced to fend off the deadly threat from the power apparatus, is at the same time summoned to life by society's strong need to hear the truth about its own fate. Such are the circumstances in Poland today. The major turning point in the consciousness of Polish society that came about at the beginning of the eighties thanks to Solidarity derived, inter alia, from the widespread realization of the need for freedom of expression. And practical conclusions were also drawn on a massive scale. Undermined from the mid-seventies onward by the individual initiatives of underground publishers, the supremacy of censorship was openly challenged in the Solidarity period by the network of independent publishing houses, distribution points and even libraries that in a short time spread throughout the country. The new consumers took avidly to the uncensored publications, whether of belles-lettres, history, current political writing or investigative journalism. Readers fed for so many years on a barren diet of censored books and censored news hungered not only for straightforward information about facts hitherto concealed, but craved an authentic artistic expression of their own experiences and ordeals. The demand grew in the grim months of martial law, disproving the old saw about the Muses being silent when the thunderous cannon roar; and this hunger has shown no signs of abating.

Over the last few years Polish literature has thus had to face a peculiar duality, poised as it is between the overt hostility of state and the inordinate expectations of society that require a writer to perform exceptionally onerous duties. The basic difficulty here is to reconcile two conflicting demands. To remain faithful to his own vocation, the writer must at the same time voice the aspirations of the public at large and the aspirations of the individual "I". By their very nature the two do not always coincide.

Janusz Anderman ranks among those Polish writers who have succeeded in finding an artistically convincing solution to the dilemma. His prose satisfies to an amazing degree the demand for a realistic picture of present-day Poland, whilst at the same time it remains an expression of the author's individualistic stance. Anderman's achievement is all the more noteworthy in that 'post-war' literature — that is to say, literature written after 1981 — has scored most of its successes in the realm of lyric poetry, which by its nature reacts more promptly to emotional upheavals and social revaluations.

Anderman's literary development to date leads in sequence to the artistic solutions that characterize his latest stories. In many respects his biography is typical for a whole generation of writers now in their late thirties, who were born and bred in People's Poland. Born in 1949, he studied Slavonic Literatures at the Jagiellonian University in Krakow. After taking his degree he worked for a short time as a reporter on the periodical *Student* (*The Student*), a bimonthly whose heyday was the early seventies. The authorities, however, soon identified it as being overly independent, and it was subjected to increased censorship. Anderman was unable to find his place in the newly-doctored *Student*. In 1976 he became involved with the underground publishing movement which was still in its infancy. Since 1978 he has been co-editor of PULS, one of the first uncensored literary periodicals to have appeared in Poland. His first two books, *Zabawa w gluchy telefon* (*Dead Telephone Games*, 1976) and *Gra na zwloke* (*Playing for Time*, 1979), were brought out by state publishing houses. But his next work, the present collection of stories, was uncensorable. In 1983 the Polish original was issued simultaneously by an émigré publisher in London and an underground printing house in Poland. From 1980 onward Anderman was actively involved in liaison work between the Union of Polish Writers and Solidarity. When martial law was declared, Anderman became a co-founder of the Committee of Aid for Internees, only to be arrested shortly afterwards himself and taken to the notorious Białołęka jail, where he spent six months. After being released he travelled for a time in Western Europe, but subsequently returned to Poland, where he is living at present.

The literary generation to which Anderman belongs grew to maturity on such traumatic experiences as the student protests of 1968, the workers' riots of 1970 and 1976, the birth of an intellectual opposition in the seventies, followed by the creation of Solidarity in 1980, and the pacification of the country by martial law (1981-83). The "Generation of '68", as it is known, yielded a rich crop of poets in the main. Its poetry and its poetic programs have contributed to one of the most dramatic areas of change in modern Polish literature. Parallel to this revitalisation and revival of poetry, interesting changes have likewise taken place in the prose of the generation, though they are numerically fewer and of a narrower scope. The movement was, however, of sufficient importance for critics in the mid-seventies (perhaps somewhat overstating their case) to have called it a "revolution of young prose".

From the moment his first work was published, Anderman was to play a prominent role in this mini-revolution. His own artistic individuality and innovation derive from his skilful manipulation and combination of two seemingly conflicting perspectives: a 'lyrical' individual point of view with ensuing looseness of narrative structure, and a reflection of reality that is realistic in the extreme, one might even say naturalistic.

The realism of dialogues in Anderman's novels and stories in particular bears an absolute stamp, and one can safely claim that, with the possible exception of Miron Bialoszewski, an extraordinary poet of the spoken language, no Polish writer before Anderman has produced heroes speaking a language so close to the authentic speech of ordinary people. This aspect of Anderman's writing is particularly difficult to preserve in translation, and the English reader should bear in mind that the dialogues in the original Polish note with the fidelity of a tape recording the language used by the man in the street today, with all its idiosyncrasies, phonetic to stylistic.

There is something more to this than literary technique or perfect authorial pitch. Like so many of the poets of his generation, Anderman sees colloquial speech as the reflection of social consciousness, in which 'folk' spontaneity combines with the distorting influences of propaganda, and concreteness and bluntness enter into peculiar marriages with the colourless bureaucratese of newspapers and television.

Anderman's dialogue technique has proved to be a particularly handy device in the stories and vignettes that depict life under martial law. It is the reality of a brutal turning point in social consciousness, a grotesquely tragic catastrophe of delusions and hopes, the reality of a historical moment in which the human collectivity stands unexpectedly before an inexorable wall of falsehood and force. The first dozen or so stories here were originally published under the Polish title *Brak tchu* (*Breathless*) — and a genuine sense of suffocation is the common experience of characters and readers alike. Anderman spares no one, comforts no one, creates no new optimistic delusions, leaves little room for hope. Hope here survives only 'behind the high prison walls' where political detainees are serving their sentences. Ordinary citizens — those tired and humiliated people who 'in the wink of an eye have learned to assume the stance of the condemned' — are bereft of it.

But for the writer hope can manifest itself in the very resilience of the human mind, preserved against all odds in the abused, maltreated language of everyday life. Even the most alien, repellent and despairing reality becomes a human reality if the intellect can find a name for it. And 'names' can range from complex literary works to the most rudimentary statements, such as the signboard (in Freeze Frame Four) announcing after the dispersal of a demonstration by tear gas, *Shop closed on account of gas*. Face to face with hopelessness, Anderman finds the only solution within a writer's reach, the only solution worthy of a writer: hopelessness must first be called by name. The problem of what is to happen next begins outside literature.

Stanisław Barańczak
Harvard University August 1985

STANISŁAW BARAŃCZAK was an award-winning Polish poet and translator who was the co-founder of KOR (the Committee for the Defense of Workers) in 1976 and was an editor of the Polish underground literary quarterly *Zapis*. From 1981-1999 he taught at Harvard University in the United States, until his retirement due to Parkinson's disease. He died in 2014.

Jerzy Pilch: The World of Janusz Anderman

The 'audibility' of Janusz Anderman's prose was noted in his first two books, *Dead Telephone Games* (1976) and *Playing for Time* (1979). Indeed, the tag 'linguistic ear' appears to have stuck to Anderman for good and all. It was apparent, albeit less ostentatiously, in his third book, *Poland Under Black Light,* which was issued underground in Poland and in Polish abroad during martial law (1983) and in 1985 in English by Readers International.

In *The Edge of the World,* his second collection of stories to be translated into English, again by Readers International, this 'audibility' assumes a new creative twist in the dialogues of his characters, their weird ripostes and aphorisms, and in the poetic, if fragmentary, descriptions. Yet, while the writer's ear faithfully registers street talk, one cannot help observing that he now commands a greater range of grotesque devices: his caricature of overheard Polish is more pronounced, and his vision of reality more extreme, than in the earlier stories.

This style and subject matter derive from wider issues. For in the years between the publication of the first two books in Poland and this new book abroad, the world —

our 'country at the edge of the world' in particular — has undergone not a few distortions and contortions. Yet can one argue that the Polish reality of the 1970s presented in *Playing for Time* was less grotesque than the Polish reality of the 1980s presented in *The Edge of the World* ? The reverse may equally well be true. Were the 1950s more grotesque than the 1980s? What was it really like then, in the days of Bolesław Bierut or in Władysław Gomulka's time? 'Grandpa,' a ten-year-old boy asks in *Poland Still?* — 'say Grandpa, what was it like in Wałęsa's time?' 'In Wałęsa's time, to be perfectly honest — the old man strains his eyes — to tell you the truth it wasn't that simple. There's more than one way. It varied like. One way and the other. That's what. Something like.'

Anderman doubtless knows that this is no answer to the boy's question. At the same time he seems to be saying that only a child can insist on an answer — or at least a funda-mental and comprehensive answer — to 'what was it like in Wałęsa's time?' Only fragmentary answers are available. One might say for instance that in Wałęsa's day, and after, Pol-ish life began to abound in picturesque collective scenes not encountered in such intensity before.

The 1980s may or may not be more grotesque than the previous decades. But one thing is evident on the landscape: the spectacle of large heterogeneous groups of people. Apart from gatherings immemorial, like shop queues and May Day parades (the balloon with the slogan *Warm Welcome to the Congress* in the story *The Three Kings* has been 'parading past the tribune for years. At the head, in the middle, a sort of symbol like. In Gierek's day, too, only it went a different route, maybe you remember…'), new throngs have sprung up, more distinctly provoked by present day events: some more or less purposeful demonstrations, more or less non-sensical chains of pure hearts, phenomena that have undoubtedly provided the inspiration for Anderman's book, and — one could even say — have become central to it.

Obvious as it may seem, this thesis must be qualified.

Firstly, it is worth noting that *Playing for Time* and *Dead Telephone Games* are also 'books about the crowd', both being based on a peculiar kind of polyphony, their texture woven from a series of monologues, dialogues, utterances, the voices of chance passersby, workmen, artists, taxi drivers and madmen. *The Edge of the World* is thus the sequel to Anderman's previous books, whose narrator paced through the spectral urban landscape, recording random 'voices of poor folk'. Nowadays his task is easier because the voices are to be heard often enough in the same place.

Secondly, the crowd in *The Edge of the World* has similarities to characters in the puppet theatre. The eye and ear of the ubiquitous narrator time and again catch the characters (or sketches of characters): the Journalist, the Provocateur, the Official, the Drunkard, the Patriot Pole, the Oppositionist Pole, the Idiot Pole. They declaim convulsively on some current issue and vanish again into the crowd.

Their language and the issues on which they pronounce are, of course, not that of the puppet theatre. Their speech is incomprehensible pulp-speak, 'rustling like dry ivy'. They make incredible calculations, ejaculate scraps of crazy arguments and declarations, tell about uncommon rituals, quote sermons, TV programs and press communiqués, relate the history of miracles and their own obsessions, attempt to stammer out some generalized truth about shop deliveries or Wałęsa. But add to this style of speech their convulsive gesticulations (paroxysms of insane laughter, shaking of fists, jerking of heads) and their grotesque costumes, and one senses again the puppet theatre.

The whirlpool of language is so swift that the need to emphasize individual issues, distinguish voices, and distribute miniature roles occasionally calls for purely external devices. Hence the rich panoply of headgear — church guards' helmets. caps with tassels, white militia caps, berets, pointed newspaper hats, cyclists' caps — with which Anderman's crowd is bedecked.

These eight stories from *The Edge of the World,* in short, offer a vision that embraces everything, from an argument about a cockroach to dialogues about Poland, from the fire at the National Theatre to the 'living photograph', and this vision is sufficiently grotesque as to be apocalyptic.

Indeed, the only act in the entire book that is not grotesque, but is natural, positive and (I apologize for the pathos) victorious, is the act of silence. In *Empty … Sort of* two writers summoned for police interrogation remain silent. And their silence, lasting many hours, brings a deeper metaphysical meaning. To paraphrase the Western woman reporter (in *Poland Still?*) attempting to formulate the essence of the event: *Silence is victory.*

The conversation between two writers, which frames the stories, is also concerned with silence (in this case, defeat). Struck for a variety of reasons with creative impotence, the two writers debate some of the consequences of 'living in interesting times'. The totality of our 'interesting times' strikes them as a panopticon, a grotesque apocalypse, as pulp-speak. They also realize that the question 'what was it like in Wałęsa's time' cannot be answered for the time being, that only a partial, fragmentary answer can be given, exemplified by individual instances such as the story of black Zmijewski or the taxi driver/mathematician. There is no guarantee, however, that individual cases will shed light on the universal obscurity.

These two writers are treated seriously by Anderman (at least, I think they are), they speak articulately and are endowed with a deep and bitter awareness of the present hour. Yet they are no different from the rest of the characters populating these pages. Nothing distinguishes them from the crowd. Or rather, nothing distinguishes the crowd from them. For the crowd also attempts to articulate some manner of truth, to escape from paralysis, to decipher at least a fragment of the new epic silence weighing upon it. This is the basis of the comedy, as well as the tragedy, in the dialogues, monologues and utterances staged by Anderman: the concrete situation in which an ordinary consumer of hotdogs finds himself contrasts with the narrator's omniscience regarding the grotesque overall picture.

In *The National Theatre's Burning Down*, a little Japanese press photographer keeps repeating 'Wałęsa, Wawel, Fibak,

Wałęsa, Wawel, Fibak', attempting to summarize in this in-
cantation all his knowledge about the country. The point,
however, is that the inhabitants of the country behave no
differently; they too attempt to encapsulate an element of
self-knowledge in some slogan, sentence, or magic spell.
Their situation is more difficult, though. The exotic visitor
has his guide books; he knows where to find basic land-
marks, is acquainted with the simplest hierarchies. They
meanwhile wander blindly among trends, values and hierarchies that have been put to rout and whose ghosts now recall unreal stage-sets. So they talk feverishly, fretfully about
cockroaches, committees and Kuroń, about defeat, victory,
television, illness and the system. No one knows what is important, and what can be given a miss. No one knows where
common sense begins, or where to find the magic formula.
'For years I could always find the key,' says one of the writers, 'it existed, it was ready-made. Now one has to write
straight.'

All this is obviously controversial. Did the key exist, or
didn't it? Should one or shouldn't one write straight, and
for that matter does Anderman write straight? One thing,
however, is beyond doubt: these stories are the perceptive
and scathing record of a consciousness tragically lost in its
quest for the Key, the Way, for Harmony; and Anderman
heightens incertitude instead of allaying it. For who knows
whether the stammering, spasmodic lamentation will really
end in an epoch of universal silence (such as there has never
been) or in an epoch of *glasnost* (which has been imminent
more than once already)?

Jerzy Pilch
Cracow, June 1988

JERZY PILCH is a novelist, screenwriter and journalist living in Poland. He is several times winner of the national Polish Nike Award.

ABOUT THE AUTHOR

JANUSZ ANDERMAN is a novelist and short-story writer, screenwriter and translator who was born in 1949 in Włoszczowa in the Kielce region of Poland. He graduated from the Jagiellonian University in Krakow with a degree in Slavic philology, having also worked as reporter on student newspapers and in radio. His work for the Polish Writers' Union in cooperation with Solidarity in 1980-81 earned him six months of detention under martial law from January to July 1982 in Warsaw's notorious Białołęka Prison, which figures prominently in his stories from Poland's martial law period.

His original prose first began appearing in the 1970s: *Dead Telephone Games* in 1976, *Hitchhiking* (under the pseudonym Marcin Czech in 1978), and *Playing for Time* in 1979. The stories of *Poland under Black Light* were banned under martial law, but appeared in Polish clandestine editions from 1983, and *The Edge of the World* in 1988. After the end of communism he continued publishing, *Prison Disease* (1992, with introduction by Tadeusz Konwicki), *Meanwhile* (1998), *Photographs* (sketches from his journalism,

2002, with updates 2007, 2010), *The Whole Time* (novel, 2006), and most recently *Black Heart* (2015).

He writes regularly for the journal *Gazeta Wyborcza*, has produced screenplays for films including the prize-winning *What am I doing here? Tadeusz Konwicki* (which he also directed, 2009), has written and translated, directed and adapted TV and live theatrical drama in Polish including the famous Czech story *Closely Watched Trains* (2017). He is a member of the Polish Film Academy. In 2011 he was awarded the Knight's Cross of the Order of Polonia Restituta. In 2010 and again in 2015 he joined the committee of intellectual and cultural figures supporting the candidacy of Bronislaw Komorowski for the presidency of Poland.

ABOUT THE TRANSLATOR

NINA TAYLOR, who also writes and publishes under the name Nina Taylor-Terlecka, is a literary historian, translator and critic who lectures on Polish Literature at the University of Oxford and at the Polish University Abroad.

Besides the stories of Janusz Anderman, her translations include an anthology of Polish Gulag poetry (PFK, 2001), a study of Polish *Heimat* literature (Presses Universitaires de France, 2002), and Jaroslaw Rymkiewicz' important testimony about the Holocaust — *The Final Station: Umschlagplatz* (Farrar, Strauss, Giroux, 1994).

ABOUT READERS INTERNATIONAL

Readers International is dedicated to making available to the widest possible English-speaking audience major works of contemporary literature from around the world.

Since 1984 Readers International has published over 50 titles representing 30 different countries of Latin America and the Caribbean, the Middle East, Asia, Africa, and Europe, featuring especially authors and works that have suffered political censorship or were written in exile.

Readers International titles from Europe include:

Janusz Anderman, *Poland under Black Light* and *The Edge of the World*, collections combined as *Poland Freeze Frames*

Maria Isabel Barreno et al., known as "The Three Marias", *New Portuguese Letters* (Portugal)

Victor Català, pseudonym of Caterina Albert i Paradís, *Solitude* (Catalonia/Spain)

Karel Čapek et al., *Literature & Tolerance* (Czech Republic)

Paul Goma, *My Childhood at the Gate of Unrest* (Romania)

Ágnes Hankiss, *A Hungarian Romance* (Hungary)

Ivan Klíma, *My Merry Mornings* (Czech Republic)

Janina Koscialkowska, *Beech Boat* (Poland)

Péter Lengyel, *Cobblestone* (Hungary)

Vladimir Makanin, *Baize-covered Table with Decanter* (Russia)

Monika Maron, *Silent Close No. 6*, *The Defector* and *Flight of Ashes* (Germany — former East)

Giorgio and Nicola Pressburger, *Homage to the Eighth District* (Hungary)

Vladimir Sorokin, *The Queue* (Russia)

Ludvík Vaculík, *A Cup of Coffee with my Interrogator* (Czech Republic)

Michal Viewegh, *Bringing Up Girls in Bohemia* (Czech Republic)